HIDDEN POWERS

The Stolen Ruby

ANDREW HOBDAY

Very special thanks to the kids for their consultation, guidance and multiple read-throughs!

Contents

Chapter 1: The Barber Shop.................................1

Chapter 2: The New Boy 10

Chapter 3: The Recruitment 17

Chapter 4: Austyn Taylor 31

Chapter 5: Meeting the Team................................. 37

Chapter 6: Practice Mission................................. 57

Chapter 7: Finding Time................................. 63

Chapter 8: Money 69

Chapter 9: No Leaving................................. 75

Chapter 10: Somebody's Following Me................. 83

Chapter 11: First Mission 89

Chapter 12: Searching for Answers 115

Chapter 13: Karim................................. 121

Chapter 14: Lightning Kid................................. 131

Chapter 15: Quick Exit 142

Chapter 16: Greg's Accident 149

Chapter 17: Dalmar's Trust 154

Chapter 18: Now or Never 161

Chapter 19: The Four 173

Chapter 20: The Clubroom....................180

Chapter 1: The Barber Shop

Jessica rushed from class towards the school gate. She had to get to her after-school job. Every afternoon, she worked at Mr. Watson's barber shop. She swept floors, cleaned mirrors, and helped customers, storing and bringing them their coats and bags. Mr. Watson was very kind, and the customers were nice to her. Most of all, she needed the money. Her family was poor. Her dad had lost his job a couple of years ago and was having trouble finding another one. Her mum was sick and couldn't work. Jessica and her younger brother, Tim, helped as much as they could.

At school, the other children teased Jessica and Tim for being poor. They called them names and kept asking why they didn't have new, fancy shoes and clothes like most other kids.

As Jessica ran from the school grounds, the bullies called out to her.

"Run, Jess. Run! Don't lose a shoe running too fast. You won't be able to buy new ones!" yelled Greg.

"Run, poor girl. Chase the five-cent coin down the road!" yelled Chloe, as she joined in the teasing.

Jessica tried to ignore them as she ran. Life was hard, and the kids made it harder. They didn't understand how Jessica and Tim had struggled over the last couple of years.

A little shop bell at the top of the door jingled as Jessica entered the barber shop. Mr. Watson looked up from the haircut he was half-way through and smiled at Jessica.

"Hey, Jess. How's it going?"

"Good. Thanks, Mr. Watson," Jessica replied. She was always careful to be cheerful at the shop. She didn't want to cause any trouble or create a fuss.

"Start with some sweeping, and then you can clean those mirrors and benches over there," Mr Watson said. He pointed to the other side of the shop.

"Yep, okay!" Jessica walked out the back to get the broom.

As Jessica started sweeping, a tall man wearing a long, dark coat walked through the door, into the barber shop.

Mr. Watson looked up. "Hello. Please take a seat, sir. I'll be with you in a few minutes." The man sat down and waited quietly as Mr. Watson finished cutting a young boy's hair. A few minutes later, he was finished. The boy's dad paid, and he and his son left the shop.

Mr. Watson walked over to the waiting, tall man. "Can I take your coat for you?"

"Yes, thank you," the man said, and handed Mr. Watson his coat.

Mr. Watson called out, "Jessica, can you please store this man's coat for him?"

Jessica lent her broom against a bench and came over to take the coat. She hung it in the small coat cupboard. Jessica kept trying to look at the man without making it obvious. He was friendly but seemed strange. His eyes kept darting around the room, from object to object. His brow was creased. His face had an expression of deep thought.

As Mr. Watson cut the man's hair, Jessica finished sweeping the floor and started cleaning the mirrors. She finished one and moved to the second. But she'd left the cleaning spray on the bench, in front of the first mirror. In a rare moment of carelessness, Jessica held up her hand in the direction of the bottle. The bottle was well out of reach, but it slid across the bench and into her waiting palm. Jessica lifted the bottle and sprayed the mirror.

Realising what she'd done, she immediately froze. Jessica kept her head still, but moved her eyes to see the tall man in the reflection of the mirror, looking at her. *Did he see what I did?*

Jessica had always felt embarrassed of her power. Thinking it was dangerous for others to know about it, she'd been careful to hide it. Only Tim and Mr. Watson had found out, and that was by complete accident. Both had promised to keep it a sworn secret.

The tall man looked back down at his lap, and Jessica cleaned the mirror in front of her. She felt her heart racing and had to concentrate to make sure she appeared calm and casual as she cleaned. Jessica was annoyed with herself. She'd always been so careful to only use her power when nobody else was around.

Mr. Watson finished up the man's haircut and they moved to the register. As the elderly barber processed the payment, he called out to Jessica, "Hey, Jess. Please bring this gentleman his coat."

"Yep," Jessica replied. She took the coat from the cupboard and brought it to the man.

"Thank you," he said as he put it on before leaving the shop.

As soon as the door shut behind him, Jessica exclaimed, "I can't believe I was so stupid!"

"How do you mean?" Mr. Watson asked.

"I used my power while that man was in the shop. Do you think he noticed? I saw him looking over at me in the mirror's reflection just after I did it. Did he act strange when he was paying?"

"I didn't notice anything in particular. I'm sure it'll be alright. But you do have to be careful. The gift you have has the potential to scare people. People are scared of what they don't understand. You know, I still remember when I first witnessed what you could do. Gee, Jess. It must have been three years ago now. You've worked to strengthen it a lot since then. Remember? You moved a page in my appointment book. The thing that stuck with me the most wasn't seeing what you could do ... it was the trust in your eyes when I swore I wouldn't tell anyone about it ... even your parents."

"You've been like a grandpa to me," Jessica said with a grateful smile.

"Your grandfather was a fine man, and a true friend of mine. I wish you had the chance to know him. He was so proud of you, Jess. I remember the day you were born. He called me up early in the morning to tell me he wasn't coming in to work. He said he was heading to the hospital for the birth of his first grandchild. Of course, he didn't need to mention it. He'd been talking about it for weeks. As soon as he rang that morning, I knew it must have been about the birth. When he came in the next day, he was so proud and couldn't stop smiling. From that day on, every customer whose hair he cut, he'd mention you. Unfortunately, you weren't even two years old when he passed away."

Walking home from the barber shop that afternoon, Jessica still felt uneasy. At one point, she even felt like she was being followed. She stopped and took a look around, pretending to check a poster in a shop window. Jessica scanned to see if anybody was following her. The footpath behind her was empty, except for an old lady walking a tiny dog. She began walking again, hurrying home.

As she opened the front door to her house and walked in, she took another look around. She didn't notice anybody and quickly shut the door behind her, making sure it was locked.

Later that night before bed, she told her brother what had happened. His reaction was predictable. He told her to stop being stupid with her power. He let his jealously show, as he did whenever she mentioned her power or used it in front of him. Sometimes she wished he had the power rather than her. Other times, she wished they both had powers. She didn't know why it had happened to her. Nobody else in the family had powers. Nobody else she'd ever met seemed to have powers. Just her. She'd discovered her power when she was seven, and for the last five years she'd been strengthening and refining it whilst at the same time trying to hide it from the world.

Chapter 2: The New Boy

Jessica's class had been kept back a few minutes after the bell. She had to dash from class to make it to Mr. Watson's barber shop on time. She managed to avoid Greg, Chloe, and the other mean students. An advantage of going to Lawson Primary School was its size. There were about a thousand students. This meant some days Jessica could use the crowd to slip out through the gate without being seen. With all those students, she'd only managed to make herself a handful of friends.

Of those, her closest friend was Tessa. She and Tessa told each other everything. They shared all of their hopes and dreams. But for some reason, she'd never told Tessa about her power. Perhaps it was to protect Tessa. As much as Jessica had strengthened and refined her special ability, it still freaked her out. She felt anyone sharing her secret may, at some point, be in danger. Then, the longer she kept the secret from Tessa, the harder it was to tell her. Jessica felt it would be awkward now, having to explain why it took years before she told her best friend.

"See ya tomorrow, Tess," Jessica said, as she paused at the front gate before starting down the road.

"See ya," Tess replied. The two girls headed in opposite directions.

That afternoon at Mr. Watson's shop was uneventful. It was busy but boring. Jessica was careful not to use her secret power at all.

"That's the last of it," Mr. Watson said as he gathered up a pile of towels for washing.

"I'm so glad it's Friday," Jessica replied. "It's been a long week." She wiped down the chair used by the last customer and took the cleaning spray and cloth over to the equipment trolley.

Mr. Watson emptied the cash register and counted out Jessica's pay for the week. "There you go, young lady. Don't go spending it all at once." He

knew she wasn't going to do that. He knew she'd
have to give most of it to her parents to help them
pay the bills. But he also knew she was fiercely
proud and didn't like being reminded of her family's
money struggles. "Thanks for your efforts this week.
I wouldn't know what I'd do without you."

"Thanks, Mr. Watson. See you tomorrow
morning," Jessica chirped, as she took the money
and tucked it deep into her pocket.

Jessica felt she was definitely being followed as
she walked down the street, past the accountants',
bakery, and café. She looked to her right and used
the glass shopfronts to check for anyone else in the
reflection.

"Hey!" somebody yelled in her direction. Jessica
whipped around to see a boy standing behind her.
Instinctively, she pressed her hand against her
pocket, where she had her money. She formed a fist
with her other hand, holding it tensely by her side.

"Don't worry. I'm not going to try and steal your
money," the boy said. He looked about her age. He
was quite tall, had blond hair, and piercing green
eyes. His fingers started fiddling with the
headphones hanging around his neck. "I saw you

coming out of that barber shop. Do you work there?" he asked.

"Just because I was there, doesn't mean I work there," Jessica replied.

"I don't know any girls that get their hair cut at a barber shop."

"Yeah, I work there," Jessica conceded. "So what?"

"Nothing. I was just curious. Do you want to get a soda before you go home?"

"No thanks," Jessica snapped. "I don't know you. I don't even know your name."

"It's Dalmar. My name's Dalmar," the boy said. "I didn't mean to scare you before. I'm sorry. I just don't know many people around here, and guessed you were about my age. I thought we could be friends."

"Sorry, I've gotta go," Jessica mumbled. She turned and walked quickly towards home. She didn't want to seem like she was checking if Dalmar was following her, so she used the reflection of shop windows and listened for footsteps until she turned the corner.

Jessica locked the door behind her and walked through the hallway, into the kitchen. She took a glass jar down from a shelf and opened the lid. She took the money from her pocket and counted it out. Jessica put twelve dollars back in her pocket and dropped the rest into the jar. She replaced the lid and put the jar back on the shelf.

She felt weird having to help support her family as a kid with the money she made from her part-time job. She found it easier to put money in the jar than handing it directly to her parents.

Jessica put her toothbrush back in the cup and rinsed her mouth. She walked out of the bathroom and down the hall. She poked her head into her brother's room. He looked up from a book.

"What's up?" he asked.

"Have you heard of anyone at school called Dalmar?" She stepped into his room. "He might be in the last year of primary school … He looks like a grade sixer. He's tall, blond, and has green eyes."

"Nah. Haven't heard of him. Is he new?"

"Not sure. I don't even know if he goes to Lawson. He might even be in year seven at high school somewhere. I don't even know if he lives around here. It was strange. He just came up this afternoon and started talking to me."

"That's a bit freaky. Anyway, I haven't heard of him." Tim looked down at his book again.

"Okay, well, goodnight."

"Yeah, goodnight."

As Jessica lay in bed, she could see a clear image of Dalmar in her mind. She had so many questions about him racing around in her head, but fell asleep soon after.

Chapter 3: The Recruitment

The sun was up, and the kitchen smelled of coffee and toast. The old radio was on, and Jessica cringed as she entered the room. It was tuned to her parent's favourite station. She hated the morning show. It was full of talking and listeners calling in. There were hardly any songs, and when one did play, it was something old.

When she finished breakfast, she left for work. Jessica didn't mind working on Saturdays. She only had to work until noon. Mr. Watson was old and very traditional. He wasn't trying to provide a service for modern customers that needed late night or Sunday haircuts. Or even Saturday afternoon ones. His shop was shut on Sundays, and he only worked until noon on Saturdays. Jessica wouldn't have to work again until Monday afternoon. That's why noon on Saturday was her favourite time of the week. She'd either go over to Tessa's place to hang out or Tessa would visit her.

Jessica was setting a good pace as she turned onto High Street. She liked to be a little early on Saturdays so she could check the muffin flavours at the bakery. She'd sometimes treat herself to a muffin before work. As she walked past the café, she noticed somebody sitting on the bench seat in front of the bakery. It wasn't strange, given it was the weekend. A lot of older people would grab something from the shops as they took their dogs for a walk and then rest a while on the seat. What was strange was to see a figure that looked her age sitting there. Even stranger, that it was Dalmar. As she approached, her mind raced. She figured she shouldn't stop for a muffin now. She should keep going until she entered the safety of the barber shop. She thought about walking past and pretending not to see him, but time ran out.

"Hey there," Dalmar said.

"Oh, hi. I didn't notice you there," Jessica lied.

"That's okay. Did you want to check the muffins or something? Do that if you want to," Dalmar said, then sheepishly looked away.

"What?" *It was really freaky that he suggested checking the muffins.* She wondered how he knew about her occasional Saturday morning treat. Perhaps just a coincidence.

"Sorry," Dalmar said. "I just figured you might have seen me here, but felt more comfortable heading straight to the barber shop. I wanted to …"

"Don't worry about it." Jessica started walking up the street.

"I don't even know your name!" Dalmar called to Jessica's back as she walked off.

"It's Jessica," she replied without turning around.

"See you, Jessica!" Dalmar yelled.

Jessica stopped dead in her tracks. It was like something took over her body. She had a few minutes before work and thought she should talk to Dalmar and get to know him. After all, he seemed friendly and innocent enough. *Am I making a big mistake talking to him? Or is it a mistake not to talk to him? I could be missing the chance to make a new friend.* She walked back to the seat and sat next to Dalmar. He smiled, sat up, and turned his body slightly towards hers. He took off his headphones and left them hanging around his neck.

"You're not a freak, are you?" she asked, immediately regretting her question. It sounded weird and rude. *I could have come up with a much better opening line.*

"Nah. I'm just a kid like you," Dalmar responded. "Hey, do you go to Lawson Primary?"

"Yeah. Do you go there? I haven't seen you. Are you new?" Jessica was so curious, she jumped at the chance to find out.

"No. I'm actually from Victor Bay."

"That's gotta be a twenty-minute drive from here. Why are you hanging around Lawson?" She wasn't only curious now, but suspicious. *What's this guy doing so far from home?*

"I'm here to talk to you, Jessica," Dalmar said in a calm and matter-of-fact tone.

Jessica began to panic. This was way too freaky, and she was feeling very uncomfortable.

"You don't have to panic," Dalmar assured her. "Do you remember seeing a man in a big coat earlier this week? He got a haircut at your barber shop?"

Usually, she'd only be able to remember a regular customer. However, because that man may have seen her power, she did remember him. But she didn't want to let Dalmar know.

"No. We get lots of customers wearing coats. How could you expect me to remember somebody with such a vague description?" she said.

"He told me you have a special gift. He told me he saw you doing something he's never seen anybody else do before." Dalmar leaned closer. "It's okay. I won't tell anyone. He won't either."

"Who are you, really? What do you want? You're really starting to freak me out." *Should I stop the conversation now? Or do I try to understand more about these strangers who know my secret?*

"I know you're sitting there trying to work out if it's better to get up and go, or stay and find out more. I did the same thing too when it happened to me," Dalmar said.

Jessica found his slight smile creepy rather than reassuring. "No. I wasn't thinking that. I was just waiting for you to explain yourself," Jessica insisted.

"Nah. I know what you were thinking. It's what I do. That's my special gift." He paused for a moment as Jessica sat frozen, her mind racing. Then he continued, "Think of a number."

She thought of the number seven but realised it'd probably be the easiest number to guess. She pictured the number seven hundred and twelve in her mind.

"Seven hundred and twelve," Dalmar said immediately. "You see, I can read your mind. I can read everyone's mind. As long as they're within about ten metres of me, I can hear every thought they have. It's hard to tune out. That's why I use these things to distract my brain." Delmar touched the headphones hanging around his neck.

Jessica didn't know how to respond. She was too shocked to say or do anything, but managed to move her mouth to form a question. "What do you and that man want with me?"

"We want you to join us. He's a recruiter. He and his team find people with special gifts and offer them jobs. They use public safety cameras and other cameras linked to the internet to look for people using their powers. Most people don't use them openly, for obvious reasons. Most people don't draw attention to themselves, so it's hard to find them. He must have heard about you from his team. He then turns up and waits until he confirms your power. Then he offers you a job. He must have felt lucky when you moved that bottle the first time he was in the shop. He had to observe me for about a month before he was sure I could read minds," Dalmar explained.

Jessica checked the time on her watch. "Oh, I'd better go. I need to start work in a few minutes. Sorry."

"I'll meet you here at noon, and we can talk more," Dalmar said.

"How did you know I finish at noon? Are you going through my mind somehow and finding that stuff out?" Jessica asked sharply.

"Nah. The sign on the door says the shop shuts at noon on Saturdays. Just figured that's when you'd finish work," Dalmar said with a laugh.

Jessica laughed too. She was beginning to like Dalmar's style.

"Okay. Meet you here at noon," Jessica agreed.

As Jessica worked, she had a chance to process what had just happened. *I just met somebody else with powers. I'm not alone. I'm not a freak. There are others out there like me.*

Jessica wasn't sure if she should tell Mr. Watson about Dalmar. There was so much to take in. So much to think through. She did her work and said nothing. She wanted to find out more before telling anyone. She didn't even know what kind of job Dalmar was talking about offering her.

At noon, she left Mr. Watson's shop and saw Dalmar sitting on the bench. An elderly gentleman was next to him, looking through some papers. Jessica walked up to Dalmar, but before she had a chance to sit, he jumped to his feet.

"Do you want to go for a walk to the park? We could chat there?" he suggested, looking sideways at the old man, keen to find somewhere more private.

"Okay," Jessica replied.

The two kids walked back up past Mr. Watson's and to the top of High Street. They crossed the road and found a quiet spot in the park where they could talk.

Jessica wasn't sure if it was the promise of a more exciting life, or the fact that she'd been holding her curiosity in the whole morning whilst working, but she was desperate to hear more about Dalmar's team and the job.

Knowing exactly what she was thinking, Dalmar got straight to the point. "Our team is made up of kids. There are other teams of adults, but ours is a specialist kids' one. All of us have at least one special gift. We train together so we can strengthen our own gifts and use them effectively together when on a mission. It's like playing in a band. It isn't enough to be a great guitar player. You have to know how to play as part of the band, so the whole band sounds good. And all of us have one of these."

Dalmar showed Jessica a watch on his wrist. It looked like any other smart watch. He swiped the screen in a special pattern, and it came to life. Now it looked nothing like any watch she'd seen before. Dalmar flicked through some of the apps. One helped you locate other team members and securely communicate with them. There was even one for ordering a car to drive you wherever you needed to go.

"That's awesome!" Jessica exclaimed.

"Yeah, it's pretty cool. So, the man you met in the barber shop is kind of like our coach. He gives us details of our missions and helps with anything that requires an adult. His name's Clint. I'm not sure if that's his real name, but that's what everyone calls him. He sends messages to us on our watches and arranges for cars to pick us up on training nights, or to meet up before missions ... I know what you're thinking .... Why am I talking about missions? Well, we do things like getting back stolen documents and finding out information from people all around the world. But there must be other teams in other countries, because most of our missions are local. It's super fun, and we get paid to do it. We train together, focusing on strengthening our own gifts once a week. We train on simulated missions once a week. We go on a real mission every three or four weeks … and no, it's not too dangerous."

Jessica wondered if she had to speak to be part of the conversation. It seemed easier just thinking all of the things she wanted to say. But she felt a bit strange letting Dalmar read her mind so much.

"Don't your parents wonder where you are every time you're training and stuff?" she asked.

"It's a bit tricky. With the teenagers' team, they mostly use the excuse of studying late at school. But it's harder for us. So, we tend to train later at night. We go to bed and then sneak out later and get back before anyone knows we're gone. From pick up to drop off, it's usually from ten to midnight. I just walk a couple of doors down the road, and one of the cars picks me up. They have really nice cars, by the way," Dalmar added.

"This whole thing—the team, the training, the missions—it's the craziest thing I've ever heard. But I want to be part of it. For the first time since I discovered I had a power, I feel like I could fit in somewhere."

"We were hoping you'd join us. I've got this for you." Dalmar slipped his hand into his jacket and brought out a watch for Jessica. "I'm glad I don't have to take this one back. I was really hoping you'd be wearing it by the end of the day."

"Whoa," Jessica said, as she took her old watch off and shoved it into her pocket. She strapped the new one to her wrist.

"Now, to unlock the screen, you have to trace out *J-1-2* over the dots, like this." Dalmar showed her how it worked. Jessica nodded as she looked on.

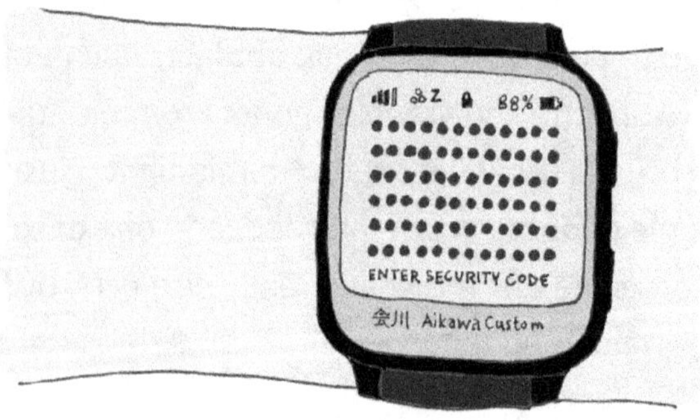

"Oh, and I know what you're thinking ..." Dalmar continued. "We get paid four hundred a week for training and practice missions. For real missions, it depends, but it's usually about three or four thousand each …. Nah, that's each person per mission … I know, it's great! They'll set you up with a bank account. Actually, you'll get two accounts. One is for your money they pay you. There's another one if you need to buy anything as part of a mission. Don't tell anyone about the accounts. You can take cash out at any ATM, so I just do that when I want to buy something …. Yeah, it'll be tricky to help your parents with this money. They'll wonder where it's coming from. You might have to get creative. Sorry, I'll try to stop reading your thoughts now …. Who am I kidding? I can't stop. Anyway, I should be going. You'll get a message on your watch sometime on Monday. That's our training night. It'll confirm the details, and there will be a car sent to collect you …. No, there aren't any contracts to sign. You just start working with us, and if you stop, you stop."

"Okay. I'll see you Monday night, Dalmar." It was all she could manage to say. Jessica was in a daze. She couldn't believe she was part of a special team of kids who went on special missions and got paid heaps of money even when they just practiced. She looked down at her new watch.

"See you Monday!" Dalmar yelled as he crossed the road and jogged off.

As she stood in the park, she realised she hadn't even checked if she was allowed to tell anyone about the team and missions. She assumed not. As Dalmar jogged up the road, he turned his head back in Jessica's direction.

"No! Nobody! None!" he yelled.

Thank you, she replied using her thoughts. She watched as he jogged up the road and disappeared around the corner. Jessica thought about how her family's financial struggles could be over—or at least make things a lot better than they currently were. She'd also have some new friends that could finally understand her awkward secret she'd kept from the world. They would have powers too. They'd probably understand how it was to feel different from everybody else, and the feeling of desperately wanting to fit in.

Chapter 4: Austyn Taylor

"Hey, Jess! Tessa's here!" a voice from the front door called.

"Thanks, Dad!" Jessica replied, and ran from her bedroom to greet Tessa.

The two girls headed straight to Jessica's room and closed the door.

"Hey! I have to show you something, Jess," Tessa said excitedly.

"What is it?" Jessica asked as both girls kicked off their shoes and sat on her bed.

Tessa dug her hand into her bag, pausing for a moment. "Who's our favourite singer? Whose songs do we know every word to?"

"Austyn Taylor!" Jessica replied in a flash, her eyes lighting up at the prospect of something to do with Austyn.

"I was over at the shopping centre, and they had a big promotion on for Austyn's new perfume for girls. Guess what I got?" Tessa pulled two small bottles from her bag and showed them to Jessica. "Mini bottles for both of us! The promo guy was handing them out. How cool!" She handed one to Jessica.

Jessica looked at the small bottle and smiled. She carefully took the cap off and smelled the perfume. It was sweet and fruity. It smelled like vanilla with a hint of strawberry.

"Thank you so much, Tessa! It smells amazing!" Jessica carefully replaced the cap. "That was so lucky. They don't usually give out samples this cool. It's such a cute glass bottle."

"This is making me think about how cool Austyn's new song is." Tessa grabbed her phone, plugged in her earbuds, and passed one to Jessica.

The girls listened to Austyn's songs for a little while, singing along into imaginary microphones.

Tessa put her earbuds and phone away. "Did you see the way Karim was looking at you in maths class yesterday?"

"No," Jessica replied. "What was he doing?"

"He was staring at you with a dreamy look … for a really long time."

"Karim does that. I've seen him do it to others. He's a bit strange, isn't he?" Jessica replied.

"Yeah. Have you talked to him much?" Tessa asked. "He's always so quiet. I don't know who he's friends with."

"He's nice. He doesn't say much, but he seems friendly. Maybe he's just shy."

"Well, the way I saw him staring at you, I think he likes you, Jess. No, wait … he may even *love* you," Tessa teased.

"Stop it," Jessica replied playfully. "He's just friendly. Karim's a nice guy. Well, actually …"

"What is it?" Tessa asked, sensing Jessica was guarding some big news.

"Nah, nothing. It's nothing. … Actually, I have to tell you what happened this morning! This guy, Dalmar was hanging out in front of the bakery. I saw him there Friday, and he said hi, but I basically ignored him. Then he was there again this morning. We chatted, and after work, we walked to the park and chatted again. He seems really nice. He's from Victor Bay."

"Victor Bay? That's ages away. What's he doing around Lawson?"

"He was just hanging out. Anyway, I don't know if I'll see him around again. Probably not," Jessica lied.

As Jessica stretched, raising her arms up, her new watch poked out from under her long-sleeve top.

"Hey, when did you get that? Why didn't I notice it before?" Tessa grabbed Jessica's wrist and pulled her sleeve up to get a better look at the watch.

"Um. I found it at a recycle store. I don't think it's a good one. It's some weird brand. It doesn't even work properly," Jessica lied. "But it looks cool, right?"

"Whoa! It's an Aikawa Custom! These are super expensive. Their processing speed's four times quicker than anything else on the market. They can be fully customised. It's like building your own watch yourself from the ground up. I've read about them, but I've never actually seen one for real. Why would anyone be selling this thing cheap?"

"The staff probably hadn't heard of the brand. They probably thought it was some rubbishy thing. Anyway, it doesn't seem to work, apart from telling the time. It really isn't worth much," Jessica lied.

Tessa tapped the screen, and it lit up. It showed a strange pattern of dots and displayed the words, *ENTER SECURITY CODE*. After a couple of seconds, it showed the time, then the screen went dark. "You'll have to do a factory reset. It'll wipe the memory, but after that, you'll be able to use it properly. I can help you," Tessa offered.

"Good idea. You really are a tech whiz. You know every brand, every device, even how to fix them,"

Jessica replied as she covered the watch with her sleeve again. *Gee! Anything tech, and Tessa's all over it. I'll have to be careful she doesn't insist on resetting the watch.*

"If you didn't think it'd work, why did you buy it?" Tessa asked.

"Nobody at school's going to know if it works or not. Especially Greg, Chloe, and the other bullies. It does show the time. Maybe if they think I can afford a smart watch, they won't tease me about being poor."

"Yeah. But try not to worry about what those losers think. They're just stupid."

"I try, but what they say gets to me. I think about what they say for hours, and I can't block it out."

Tessa pulled her perfume bottle out of her bag. She took off the lid, covered the opening with her finger, and tipped it up. She leant over and tapped her wet fingertip onto Jessica's neck. "There you go. Now you're protected from bullies by this special Austyn potion." She smiled warmly.

"Thanks, Tessa. You're an amazing friend."

Chapter 5: Meeting the Team

Jessica sat at the dining table eating the usual Monday night dinner. Jessica's dad cooked pasta on Mondays. "More pasta, less meat" was his motto. He said the cheaper he could make dinners early in the week, the more chance of having something fancier on the weekend. At least, that was his theory.

"Anything exciting happen at school today, Timmy?" their dad asked.

Tim lifted his head, a piece of spaghetti hanging from his mouth. He slurped it up, then answered, "Nah."

"How about you, Jess? Anything interesting?" he continued.

"Nah, not really."

Jessica finished dinner and went to her room to draw for a while before bed. She'd been into drawing Japanese manga art for about three years and had a real talent for it. She sat at her desk, adding colour to a picture of a warrior—a fierce-looking girl with long blue hair, holding a sword above her head. As she carefully added some orange to the girl's wrist armour, Jessica's watch buzzed. It was asking her to enter the security code. She ran her fingers over the strange pattern of dots the same way Dalmar had showed her. There was one message waiting to be read. It was from Clint:

> *Training tonight. Driver will pick you up at 9:40 p.m., two doors up the street from your house. When you get here, your watch will ask you for a code. Put in the code you just used to unlock the watch, and a door will open to a building. That's where you'll meet the team.*
>
> *See you tonight.*
>
> *Clint.*

Jessica's heart started to race with excitement.
She'd forgotten about Monday being training night.
She'd been so caught up in her boring Monday,
she'd totally forgotten about her new, secret life.
She went to the bathroom and cleaned her teeth.
On the way back to her room, she said goodnight to
the rest of the family. Then she changed into some
black tracksuit pants and a black windcheater. She
put her pyjamas over the dark clothes, set a small
alarm clock for 9:30 p.m., shoved it under her
pillow, turned off the light, and crawled into bed.

She woke to the alarm's muffled tone in her ear.
She frantically pressed it to stop the noise before
anyone in the house heard it. She quietly slipped
out of bed, replacing her shape under the blankets
with some cushions. Jessica wasn't too concerned
about her parents discovering she wasn't in bed.
She knew they didn't check on her often. When they
did, they'd only step into her room.

Jessica slowly slid her window open and removed
the flyscreen, gently lowering it to rest on the
ground outside her window. She climbed out onto
the grass, turned around, and slid the window back
to where it was almost shut again. From a distance,
anyone would think it was shut. Her watch buzzed,

and she froze. She looked down and saw it was asking for her code to be entered. She entered it and read a new message:

Your car is now approaching. Number plate 2AX4EV. Driver's name is Zac.

She ran across the front yard through the open driveway gates. Checking momentarily that nobody was around, she ran two doors up and saw a car pulling over on the other side of the road. She checked the number plate before opening the back door and climbing in. A small, interior light came on, and the driver turned to greet her.

"Good evening, young lady. My name's Zac, and I'll be your driver for tonight." Zac looked middle-aged and had kind, chocolate-brown eyes. His hair was a bit scruffy, and he had a short, well-kept beard. He turned back to the steering wheel, and as soon as Jessica had put her seat belt on, he started to drive.

Jessica kept track of the time using her watch, and after around twenty minutes, Zac turned into a driveway. It was part of an industrial estate, made up of many factories and office buildings. Zac parked in one of the car spaces in front of a factory door. Jessica noticed several other cars were already parked in spaces nearby.

Zac turned to face her. "We're here, young lady. I'll be waiting for you to finish, and I'll take you back home. Any problems, you can call me on your watch. I'm the only Zac, so just look me up in the team list."

"Thanks, Zac. See you later." Jessica opened the car door and climbed out. As she slowly approached the factory door, she could hear the gravel under her feet. It seemed so loud and echoed into the night. Recalling Clint's instructions, she looked at her watch. It displayed the words, *ENTER SECURITY CODE*. She put in her code, and the watch unlocked. The screen flashed green three times, displayed the time for a couple of seconds, then went dark. A small light turned on near the bottom of the factory door. It shone onto the concrete square in front of the doorway. The door slowly slid to one side. Jessica was nervous. Although this was what she'd been expecting, the factory looked so broken down from the outside. It looked like it was about to fall apart. She wondered how it could possibly be a good training centre.

Jessica walked through the doorway and along a narrow corridor. It was lit with dull red lights. She heard the front door slide shut behind her and the sound of a lock snapping back into position. She got to the end of the corridor, and another door slid open. Jessica couldn't believe what she saw. She looked around a huge, well-lit room. It was like a brand-new building. There was equipment everywhere. One corner had gym equipment. There were bikes, treadmills, and weights. Another area had obstacle-course-type equipment, with ropes, cargo nets, climbing frames, and a rock-climbing wall. There was a corner filled with weapons. Some she didn't even recognise, but she did see spears, staffs, nunchaku, sai, throwing stars, and blow pipes. The last corner had whiteboards on the walls and a bunch of beanbags scattered on the ground. There also seemed to be several rooms leading off from the huge training room. As Jessica took another look around, she noticed movement from the beanbags. She couldn't see anyone there before, but now she could see some kids about her age getting up from where they sat. She heard the door behind her open again and looked back to see another kid enter the room. Glancing to the far side of the training room, she saw the man who had been in Mr. Watson's a few days ago. He strode towards her, smiling slightly.

"Hello, Jessica. Remember me? I'm Clint," he said. "Welcome to our training centre. I'll introduce you to the rest of the team."

Three kids walked over from the bean bags and stood next to Clint. The kid who'd walked into the training room just after Jessica came around to join the others. There were two more kids walking out of the same door Clint had appeared from, one of them Jessica recognised as Dalmar. They both joined the others. The whole team stood in front of her. They introduced themselves one at a time.

"You know me already," Dalmar began. "I'm Dalmar. I'm twelve years old, and I read minds." He gave her a slight nod and a friendly smile.

Next was an older-looking boy with short, curly, red hair and light hazel eyes. "I'm Joseph. I'm thirteen, and I can move ten times quicker than the average person."

Joseph | Age: 13
Power: x10 faster

A girl stepped forward. She had long, straight, black hair and brown eyes. "I'm Jade. I'm thirteen. I can hypnotise people and erase their short-term memories." Jade stepped back.

Jade | Age: 13
Power: Hypnotism /
short-term memory

A boy spoke next. He had black hair and olive-green eyes. "My name's Nikhil. I'm eleven years old. My special gift is invisibility." Jessica was drawn in by his eyes. They had the intensity of a lion's. It wasn't that they were scary or menacing. They were simply piercing.

Nikhil | Age: 11
Power: Invisibility

"I'm Brooke," a girl with short, brown hair and dark brown eyes said, as she lifted her head to stare straight at Jessica. "I'm thirteen years old, and I'm the strong one. They've measured me at sixteen times the strength of a fully grown, physically active adult."

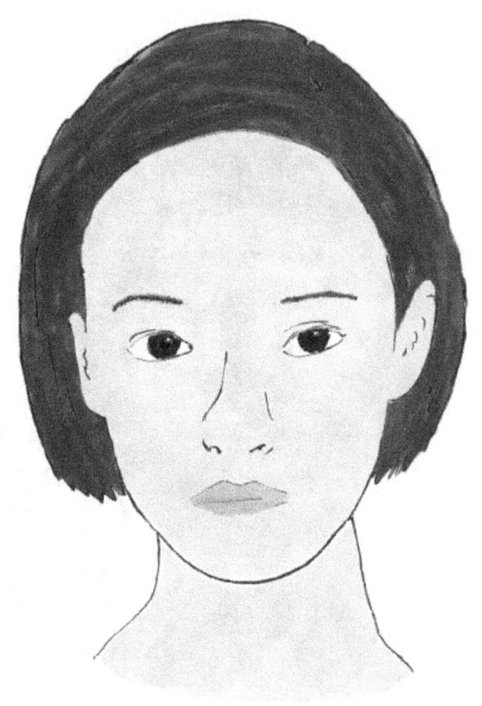

Brooke | Age: 13
Power: x16 stronger

The last to step forward was Kai. He had messy black hair, partially covering his face, and brown eyes. He looked a bit like some of the manga characters Jessica had drawn. He had a coolness about him, like he was too cool to care how he looked. "I'm Kai. I'm eleven years old. I can teleport over short distances. It's kind of fun."

Kai | Age: 11
Power: Teleportation
over short distances

Now that the whole team had introduced themselves, Jessica felt she had to do the same. "I'm Jessica. I'm twelve years old. I can move things with my mind."

"Thanks, team," Clint said. "Everyone can start now. Thirty minutes on individual work, then another thirty in pairs. Swap pairs and do another thirty, then we'll finish with some weapons and extra skills work. Okay, let's go." With that, everyone moved off to different areas of the training room, seemingly familiar with the night's routine.

Clint motioned for Jessica to follow him to the weapons area. "Everyone has a special gift, but we like to expand the team's skills. Everyone trains with one or two weapons and picks up other specialist skills. I want you to fill a couple of gaps we have. We need somebody to train with the sai. By the way, it's like the word 'sheep'. Whether you're talking about one sai or two, you just say, 'sai.' There's no 's' on the end. They're a slick weapon. Oh, and the whole team train with throwing stars too. They're called, 'shuriken.' There's no 's' on the end of 'shuriken' either."

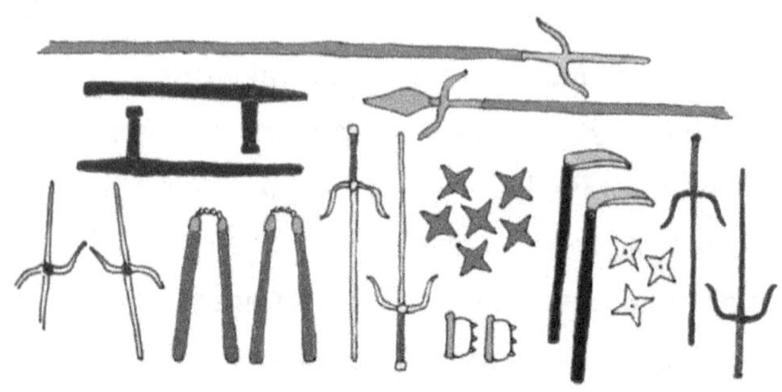

He walked over to a wall of weapons and picked a pair of sai from it. He took Jessica's hand and moved her forearm so that it was facing him. He then held one of the sai against her forearm, using it to compare the length. He stepped back over and placed them on the wall and took another, slightly shorter pair.

They weren't the shiny chrome she was used to seeing in martial arts movies. The metal was black and dull. The middle prong was the longest, and the prong on each side curved out slightly at the ends. The handles were wrapped with a leather binding, and there was a short cylinder-shaped end underneath the grip.

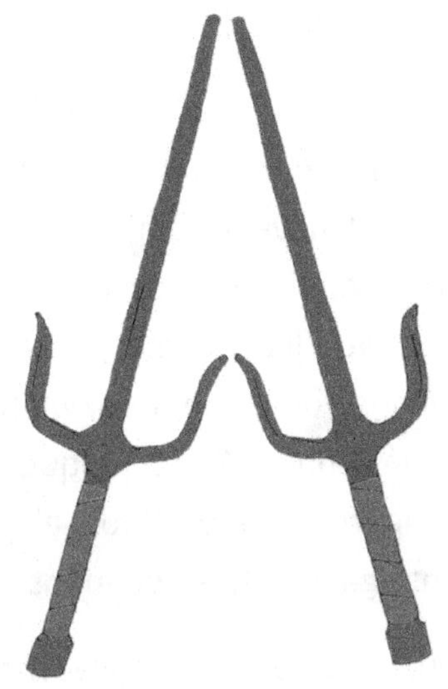

Clint took Jessica's hand again, and she faced her forearm to him. He checked the sai's length and nodded. He gave her the pair of sai. Jessica couldn't help smiling. *It feels so awesome to be holding such a cool weapon! But they're heavier that I thought they'd be.*

Clint pointed to the middle prong of the weapon. "These are a perfect fit. They're meant to be just a little longer than your forearm." It extended a slight bit past Jessica's elbow. He then motioned for Jessica to move over to the area of the training room with the beanbags, whilst holding onto the sai. He opened a cabinet and took out a black, cloth bag.

"Store your sai in here. You'll need to train with them every day. I'll have a training program including instructional videos uploaded to your profile. It means you'll be able to access them on your watch. When you come here, we have some trainers that can refine your technique, so you're not just learning from videos. You'll also get a chance to fight against other weapons."

"Thank you." Jessica wasn't sure what else to say. She felt she had to say something but was still so dazed by all she'd seen.

Clint opened another cabinet and took out a small, leather pouch. He spread the contents onto the top of the cabinet.

"These are lock picks. If used by somebody with enough skill, this set will get you into most locks you'll find on any given mission. We used to have a master lock-picker, but he's moved into another team. We need to fill the gap, so I want you to learn how to use these. The same thing applies. Take them home, and I'll load up some videos you can access on your watch." Clint placed the pick set into another cloth bag.

He held up a small wooden board. "This is a practice board. It has three locks on it that you can try to pick." He placed the practice board into the bag for Jessica.

Clint then opened another cabinet. He took out two books and handed them to her.

"Japanese?" Jessica said. "But I learn Mandarin at school, and I'm not very good at it."

"Yes. I want you to learn Japanese. We find it helps if the team knows some languages between us all. We have interpreter and translator apps on the watches, but nothing's quite like having somebody that can speak the language on a mission. We have a gap with Japanese, so I want you to learn that specific language. Don't worry, we don't expect you to be fluent straight away. It'll take some time. Your watch will have most of the learning material you need, but we find giving kids a couple of books helps if parents start asking questions. Just tell them you have an interest in the language and decided to give it a try." Clint put the books into a third cloth bag and handed it to Jessica.

Jessica was extremely overwhelmed. She wondered how she'd be able to do all this extra practice and study each day. She already went to school, worked for Mr. Watson six days a week, and helped out around the house. She didn't want to give up her artwork, as that made her happy.

Clint sensed she was overwhelmed. "Don't worry. Everyone finds it all a bit much in their first week. Give it time. You'll work out how to balance it all."

For the rest of the training session, Jessica moved around the room, looking at all the equipment. She was free to explore as the others completed their set tasks then paired up. Jessica spent some time looking at her two sai, running her fingers over the cold steel. She put the sai back in their bag and opened the bag with the lock picking set. She unsnapped the pouch's button and took the tools out.

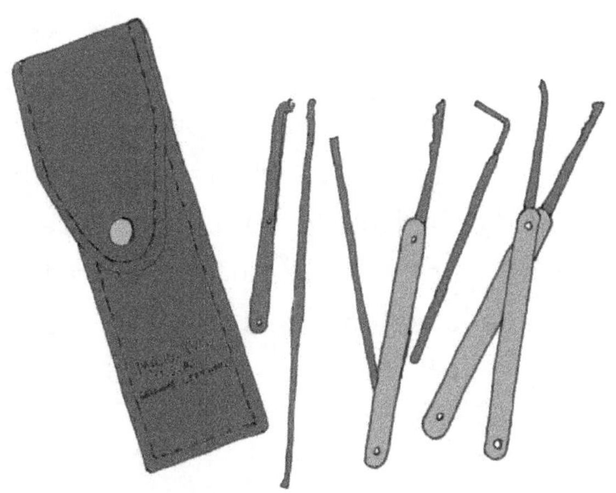

Most of them looked similar. They had handles that looked like popsicle sticks. They narrowed from the handles to the heads. Each head was a different shape. Some of them looked like the teeth of a saw you'd use to cut wood. There were also some L-shaped pieces of metal in the kit. She put them back in the pouch and into their bag.

Before the session was over, Dalmar came up to Jessica to check on her. "The first night can be really full on. You'll get used to it though," Dalmar reassured her.

Jessica crept across the lawn to her bedroom window. She kept checking to see if anybody was around, and then slid the window open and climbed through. She carefully replaced the flyscreen from inside her room and slid the window closed again. She kicked off her shoes, stashed all three cloth bags under her bed, threw the cushions aside, and crawled in under the covers. She was so tired and had to get up for school in less than seven hours.

Chapter 6: Practice Mission

The rest of the week flew by. Jessica had established a new pattern. She'd still go from school to Mr. Watson's barber shop. Then she'd go home and eat dinner. But after dinner, she'd now train with her sai, lock picks, and language videos and books. Every night she pushed herself to learn a new technique with the sai, pick a lock quicker than before, and memorise ten new Japanese words. Monday and Thursday nights at ten o'clock were training and practice missions at the training centre. Friday and Saturday nights she'd treat herself to some manga artwork time.

Saturday at noon, Jessica headed home after working the morning at Mr. Watson's. It was her turn to visit Tessa's house this week, so she was going to do some quick sai training, revise some new Japanese words and phrases, and then walk to Tessa's.

Jessica lay on her bed scrolling through a list of words on her watch. She read each word in English first, then tried to recall the Japanese equivalent, before checking to see if she was right. She was so tired that her eyelids grew heavy and she fell asleep for around an hour, before waking up in a panic. Now running late for Tessa's, she quickly got ready, rushed down the hallway, and yelled out to her parents, "I'm going to Tessa's now! Back later!"

Tessa opened the door to see Jessica standing there, breathing heavily, having half walked, half jogged to get there.

"You're late. What happened?" Tessa asked.

"Sorry, Tess. I fell asleep. I was so tired. I've …"

"What?" Tessa asked, curious to hear more.

"I was actually practicing some Japanese words. I'm trying to learn the language. I was lying on the bed and got really tired and fell asleep."

"Japanese? Wow. Good for you. I struggle enough with learning Mandarin at school. I thought you did too?"

"I do. I find Mandarin hard. I don't think I'm a language person. But I just wanted to give Japanese a try. We'll see. I'll probably give up in a week." Jessica tried to make it sound like it was only her curiosity that motivated her to start learning.

Jessica felt terrible keeping the truth from Tessa. She'd always told Tessa everything ... except about her special power. Now it was the same power that was causing her to lie and hide more from Tessa. Jessica wondered how bad it would be just to tell one person about the secret team. But she decided not to tell Tessa, at least for now.

It was Thursday night and over a week and a half since Jessica had started training. She lay in bed, her pyjamas covering her black pants and dark navy hoodie. As she waited for the time to leave, she thought about all that had happened since joining the secret team. She was tired all the time and knew she had to give up the job at Mr. Watson's. There was no other way to survive the intense training schedule. She was also wondering when she'd see any money from her new job. She hadn't been told anything further about being paid and felt too awkward asking Clint.

Jessica entered the training centre, ready for another practice mission. When the team had all arrived, Clint gathered them around.

"Tonight, we're practicing the retrieval of a stolen gem. It's being held in a secure location." Clint pointed to a small table pushed against the wall, just to the side of the gym equipment. On the table was a red-coloured gem, covered by a square plastic case. "You'll need to run on the treadmills, scale the cargo net, move along the rock-climbing wall, deactivate the alarm and lasers, open the locks, and grab the gem."

Each team member jumped on a treadmill and set it to a running pace. After a ten-minute run, they moved through the obstacles. Coming to the alarm and lasers, Joseph used his super speed to get to work. He was able to move ten times as quickly with activities like running, kicking, and punching, but also with delicate tasks like deactivating alarm systems and lasers. Joseph had developed a specialist skill in this area. He unzipped a small toolkit and started unscrewing the front of the security system. He moved so fast it was hard to keep up with what he was doing. In less than a minute, the lasers and alarm status lights turned off.

"Done," Joseph said with a loud whisper.

Jessica used her powers to move the clear cover protecting the ruby. This meant nobody would see any finger prints after the team had gone. She then set it down on the table, next to the ruby. She focused on the gem, moving the ruby to a bag Nikhil was holding open. With the ruby inside, he turned invisible and carried it to Kai. Kai took the bag and teleported himself and the bag to the other side of the room and handed the bag to Clint.

"Mission complete! Well done, team," Clint said. "Very well done indeed. Of course, I could have made it simpler. But it was important to practice your special gifts as a team, and in a way that you could do this mission in a large building."

The team ran through a few variations of the mission, incorporating some of their other special gifts and talents.

"Great session, team!" Clint praised them again. "See you all Monday."

The kids grabbed their bags and backpacks from the beanbag area and headed to the door. The room was filled with the sound of clunking metal as weapons moved around in the bags as they were hoisted onto shoulders.

"Hey, Jessica!" Clint called, "I almost forgot. Here are your accounts and debit cards." Clint handed Jessica a thick cardboard envelope.

"Thanks," Jessica replied as she took the pack.

As soon as Jessica had hidden her sai and lock picks under her bed, she ripped open the envelope Clint had given her. She found some papers explaining when and how to pay for mission costs. Most of it was to do with overseas missions. She looked at the plastic cards. There was one with a company name, *Solutions Corporation*. That was the one for mission costs. The other card had her name on it. It was her bank account where she'd get paid. She couldn't wait to get to the bank the next day to check if she had money in her new account.

Chapter 7: Finding Time

Friday was tough for Jessica. She was exhausted from training all week. She almost fell asleep in class. Working at Mr. Watson's was easier, but she had to make sure she kept moving around and working to stay awake.

On the way home, she crossed to the other side of High Street and stopped at the bank. She took her new card out of her purse and inserted it into the ATM.

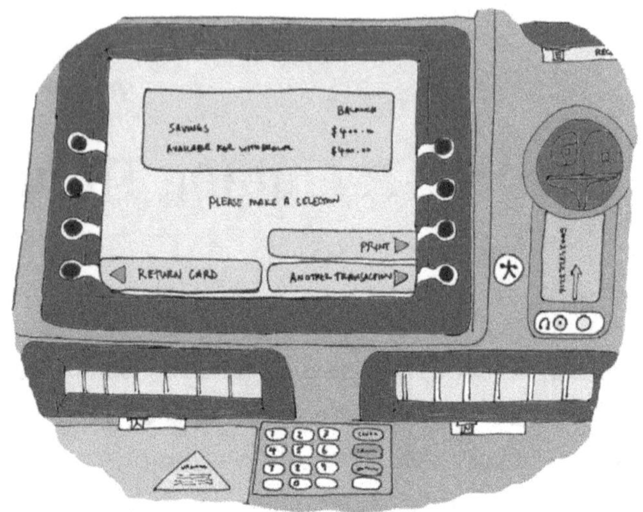

She checked the account balance. It showed four hundred dollars on the screen. In a few days, there would be another four hundred for her second week of training. She stared at the screen. *This changes my life. This changes my family's life.*

That night, Jessica thought about how she was going to survive training each week, keep her new job a secret, and help her family with more money than before without being questioned about where it was coming from.

I have to quit the barber shop. I can't work there six days a week and train as hard as I need to. I'm not getting enough sleep. If I quit, I could train in the afternoons and sleep at night. I'd only have two late nights a week—Mondays and Thursdays. At the moment, every night's a late one with sai, lockpick, and Japanese practice. But if I quit, who's going to help Mr. Watson? And how do I explain making more money than ever before without working? If I pretend to keep working for Mr. Watson, I could train in his back room. But then I'd have to tell him about the secret team. Or perhaps I could tell him I wanted to learn new skills instead of earn money ... hang on ... I've got it! How brilliant! I quit the barber shop and tell everyone I'm selling manga artwork for heaps of money. That way I can spend plenty of time in my room with the door shut. I can practice sai and pretend to be drawing art. But who's going to help Mr. Watson? I wonder if anyone at school wants a part time job ...

As Jessica walked up High Street towards the barber shop, she'd decided what to do. She was going to tell Mr. Watson she needed a break from her job there, so she could concentrate on her art.

"Good morning, Jess." Mr. Watson beamed. He was very bubbly for an early morning.

"Good morning, Mr. Watson." She decided to talk to him before customers started coming through the door for their Saturday morning appointments.

"I wanted to talk to you about something," Jessica said gingerly.

"Of course. What's on your mind?"

"I need to take a break from working here. I really love working with you, but I need more time for my artwork. I'm starting to sell some of it," Jessica lied. "And between school and working six days a week, I just can't fit everything in."

Mr. Watson looked visibly disappointed. He wanted Jessica to be happy, but he really enjoyed her company. Also, having her in the shop reminded him of her grandfather, who he missed very much.

"Well, Jess, if that's what you need to do, then of course I'll support you. I might even get a couple of those artworks for the shop wall ... before you get too famous and they cost too much for me to afford," Mr. Watson said with a smile. He still looked disappointed but was trying his best to support her decision.

"But what about the shop? Who's going to help with the sweeping, the cleaning, the other things I do? I can ask around at school? There might be somebody interested," Jessica offered.

"It's okay, Jess. A couple of my grandchildren can help me out for a while. I can work out what to do after that. Maybe you can let me know in a few weeks if you want to come back before I offer it permanently to anyone else?"

"That'd be good. Who knows if this art thing will work out?" Jessica agreed. She hated keeping the lie going, but she wasn't able to come up with a better way to deal with the situation.

"Actually … do you think you could help me with something?" Mr. Watson asked. "I can cover most of your shifts, but there's one I know I'll struggle with. Do you think you could do the next couple Friday afternoons? It's just until I sort that day out? I may even shut early on Fridays. Goodness knows, I need to slow down a bit and move towards retirement."

"No problem. I can definitely help out with the next few Fridays," Jessica agreed. She felt terrible. Mr. Watson was even considering shutting earlier on Fridays, and all because of her. She hoped he was being honest about needing to move towards retirement and that it wasn't just something he said to make her feel better.

As Jessica cleaned the last mirror and chair, Mr. Watson sharpened a pair of scissors he'd been using.

"You know, Jess. I'll be okay from next week, so you don't need to come in Monday. But if you can do those Fridays, that'd be much appreciated."

"Thanks. And yes, I'll be here Fridays. It'll be nice to spend time in the shop," Jessica said with a smile.

As Jessica left the shop that afternoon, she felt a sense of loss. As much as her new, secret job was exciting and paid lots of money, she'd enjoyed working in the barber shop immensely.

Chapter 8: Money

"Jess, it's time for breakfast. Otherwise, you'll be late for work!" Jessica's dad called from the kitchen. Jessica figured it was too hard to explain what was going on by calling back. She had to get out of bed.

"I'm not going to work today," Jessica said sleepily as she entered the room.

"What do you mean?" her dad asked.

"It's Sunday. Mr. Watson doesn't open on Sunday."

"Ah, yes. How did I forget?"

"But I do have some news. It's about the days I work." Jessica paused for a second and took a breath, "I'm only going to be working at Mr. Watson's on Fridays from now on."

"What happened? Is he okay? He isn't retiring yet, is he?"

"Everything's fine. I've just been able to sell some of my artwork, and I want to focus on creating more of it. That's all."

"Who's buying it? Where are you selling it?" Jessica's dad probed with a sense of concern.

"It's alright, Dad. Don't worry. The manga drawing club connects undiscovered artists with art dealers and distributors. They liked my work and sold one. They said they could sell a lot more if I was able to create enough pieces per month to make it worth representing me."

"I'm your dad. You're twelve years old. It's my job to worry about you," Jessica's dad insisted.

"If I focus on my art, I can make a lot of money for the family. I just want to be able to help us, Dad. That's all," Jessica said.

"Okay. Well, if anything doesn't feel right … like the art dealer people or anything, you just let me know. I want you to know you can ask me for help. I really appreciate all you're doing for the family. It's been such a tough couple of years with Mum being sick and all, and me losing my job. I feel so bad I can't give you all the things you deserve and be the one looking after you with money ... rather than you helping all of us out with your money. I'm so sorry it's like this, J-bear. I promise it'll get better." Her dad wrapped his arms around her and held her tight.

"It's okay, Dad. I know you're doing your best. I really do," Jessica reassured him.

It was Tuesday afternoon, and Jessica headed home from school. She detoured up High Steet to stop at the bank. She inserted her card into the ATM. Her account balance was now eight hundred dollars. *Yes! It's gone up from the four hundred yesterday when I checked. Tuesdays must be payday for the week before. Tuesday could now be my favourite day of the week. I've never seen this much money in an account with my name on it! Actually, I've never seen this much money in an account on a screen before.* Jessica withdrew five hundred dollars, quickly slipped it into her purse, and walked the rest of the way home.

Jessica couldn't wait to put the money into the family jar her parents relied on. She took the jar from the shelf and opened the lid. She took the money from her purse and counted it out. The fifty-dollar notes from the ATM were in a separate part of her purse, so she didn't really need to count them. But she wanted to feel what it was like to hold five hundred dollars. She dropped the wad of notes into the jar and replaced the lid. They unrolled, pressing up against the inside of the jar.

Jessica sat in class, daydreaming. She'd finished her maths exercises and had a few minutes of free time. A week had now passed since she'd drawn the five hundred dollars out of the bank and put it into the money jar. Her dad had been very surprised to see so much money. He didn't say anything directly to Jessica, but she could feel his appreciation though little smiles and extra-long hugs. It made her feel good to be helping out, but she was worried. She still hadn't been on her first mission. The training and practice missions were fun. She was excited about how well she could fight with sai and pick locks. She'd even impressed herself with how well she was learning a new language. But it puzzled her why she'd need to know how to fight with weapons for a mission. And why anyone in the team would need to speak Japanese. She decided to ask Dalmar on Thursday about the missions he'd been on. She wanted to know where they'd been and how dangerous they were.

On the way home, she withdrew another five hundred dollars and put it in the jar when she got home.

Later that night, Jessica was sitting in her room at her desk. She was practicing with her lock picks. She'd been given another practice board with three new locks earlier in the week and had already picked two of them. She heard a knock.

"Jess. Can I come in?" Jessica's dad asked.

"Sure, Dad. Hang on." Jessica quickly pushed the board and picks under a jumper and slid a piece of half-finished art in front of herself. She'd rehearsed this for times when somebody came into her room while she was practicing. She got up and opened the door.

"Sorry to disturb you, J-Bear," her dad said. "I just want to ask you something. The money that you've been putting in the jar … is that from your artwork?"

"Yes. Of course," Jessica lied.

"Ah, okay. I just wanted to check. It's a lot of money. It's amazing that you're selling so much of your art. It's really good, so I can understand why plenty of people want to buy it. I just didn't think there'd be a way of selling so much of it."

"I'm surprised too. The art dealer just keeps selling it. I can't keep up," Jessica lied again.

"Okay, well I'll let you get back to it. I really appreciate what you're doing for the family. Most girls your age would be out spending any money they had on themselves. Make sure you keep some of it and buy something nice every so often, alright?" Her dad gave her a smile. "Goodnight, J-Bear."

"Goodnight, Dad."

Chapter 9: No Leaving

After Thursday night's practice mission ended, Jessica pulled Dalmar to the side before he left.

"Hey, Dalmar. I need to talk to you about something."

"Not here," Dalmar whispered under his breath. He put his arm around her shoulder and spoke more loudly, "You tired out there, Jessie-girl? Looks like you had a full-on training session tonight. You and your star lock-picking performance."

Jessica realised what he was doing and played along. "Yeah, it was pretty full-on. But fun. You sat back and did nothing, you lazy thing," she teased.

The two walked out of the training centre and into the carpark. As the other kids left the centre and walked to their cars and drivers, Jessica and Dalmar stood and continued to talk casually. When the others were gone, Dalmar asked quietly, "What did you want to talk about?"

"I want to know about the missions. What are they like?" As soon as she'd finished talking, she remembered that Dalmar could read minds. Of course. He knew what was on her mind. Although, he tended to let people say things so he didn't slip up and reveal his powers accidently. He also found it a bit rude to jump in, based on reading minds, even if he was speaking with people who knew he could do it.

"I'd better get going," Dalmar said. He knew his driver was getting curious as to why the two kids weren't getting into their cars to go home.

Jessica suggested a time when they could chat using her thoughts. *We could talk after I finish work at Mr. Watson's tomorrow afternoon. Not sure if you know I only do one shift a week there now? Anyway, do you have time tomorrow afternoon?*

"Absolutely, Jessica," Dalmar confirmed, as he turned and walked towards his waiting driver.

As agreed, Dalmar was waiting for Jessica on Friday afternoon, as she left Mr. Watson's barber shop. They decided to head to the park for a short while before Jessica had to go home.

"I need to know," Jessica said, wasting no time to ask her questions, "if the missions aren't dangerous, why are we spending so much time training with weapons? Do they all happen in this city, or do we need to travel? And how do I leave the team if I get sick of lying to everybody I care about?"

Dalmar answered one question at a time. "Yeah, the missions can be dangerous. Sometimes we have to travel to different cities, and sometimes different countries. And you can't leave the team."

"But when we first met, you told me missions weren't dangerous. You told me I could leave whenever I wanted ... they were all lies," Jessica snapped.

"I had to say those things. We all get told that stuff."

"Someone must have left some time. There are so many reasons why people would need to leave," Jessica insisted.

"Only when you've been with them long enough that they trust you. They need to trust you won't share all of their secrets. Umm, I think it's the role of the team coach to decide if you're trusted," Dalmar explained.

"Has anyone left before they're trusted?"

"I've been there for almost a year, and I only remember one guy leaving. He was lazy. He struggled with training. He wasn't getting better. One day he just stopped turning up. Clint was so annoyed. Apparently, the guy told his parents about the team and how we all have magical powers. Of course, his parents told the police, and when they turned up to the training centre, the place was just a broken down, old factory. You see, they'd removed all the stuff inside and put some broken furniture in there. So, the police didn't believe the kid. They thought he was just trying to get attention. That was the last time we moved locations. It was a few months ago now. When it happened, I remember on the night of training, my driver just took me to the new building. I went in thinking it'd be different somehow. I thought it'd be obvious why we relocated—like, for more room, a better kitchen, something. I thought somebody would explain it to us. But Clint said nothing, and nobody felt okay to ask …. It just felt like something we weren't meant to talk about. I did read somebody's mind at the time to find answers. It was one of the specialist weapons trainers who must have known what had happened. I didn't find out much. But I know Clint closed the guy's bank account and took back the money in it. Clint got some hackers to make it look like the guy's account never existed."

"What? Why didn't the police try a bit harder? I mean, the kid would have impressed them with his powers. That'd help them believe something was going on."

Dalmar shook his head. "Nah. His special gift was knowing when another person had a gift and kind of what it was. Not exactly what it was, but close enough to be helpful. So, without a factory full of evidence, it just seemed like he was making up a bunch of lies about gifted people. None of us want to have our secrets discovered by the police, so if he did try to tell, we'd just deny it."

"Doesn't seem much of a gift. I mean, it's okay, but how could he help a team's mission? Everyone already knows each other's powers," Jessica said.

"A while back, we came across some others on a mission. They were trying to take the same gold and silver bars we were. That guy told us they had gifts. Clint was very interested in finding out more. Perhaps that was why he was annoyed when the guy left our team."

"Whoa … so, there's another team running around out there with powers?" Jessica asked.

"Hey, you can calm down. Heaps of gifted people are probably running around. Some will do what we do, I guess. Don't worry about it. As long as we do our missions, that's all we need to care about," Dalmar reassured her.

Jessica wanted to press Dalmar for more details, but he'd already made it clear that she was stuck in the team for a while longer at least. She was just hoping the missions wouldn't be anything too crazy.

"I'd better go now," Jessica said. "It's almost dinner time. Thanks for the chat. I'll see you next week at training."

"No problem. Hope that helped. See you Monday," Dalmar replied.

"Dinner!" Jessica's dad called from the kitchen.

Jessica and Tim came into the room and grabbed a plate each.

"Is Mum going to join us?" Tim asked.

"I think she's resting, mate," their dad answered. "But you can check on her if you like."

"I'll go!" Jessica jumped in. She headed to the parents' bedroom. She knocked gently on the open door as she walked in. Her mum opened her eyes and looked over.

"Hi, Jess. How are you, honey?" her mum asked.

"I'm okay, Mum. How are you feeling? Are you hungry?"

"I'm okay, sweetie. But I don't think I'll have anything to eat at the moment. Maybe later. I'll see how it goes," Jessica's mum said wearily.

"I'll pop a plate in the fridge for you. Do you need anything? Anything to drink?"

"No thanks, hun. I just need to get a bit more rest." She adjusted her pillow, turned her head a little, and smiled at Jessica.

"Okay. I'll check on you before I go to bed."

"Thanks, Jess."

Chapter 10: Somebody's Following Me

"Jess! Tessa's here!"

"Okay, Dad!" Jessica yelled back. She quickly packed up her sai and shoved them under her bed. She grabbed her backpack and ran to the front door.

"We're going to the shopping centre, Dad. We'll be back at about two," Jessica said as she beamed at Tessa. She hugged Tessa, and the two girls walked up the driveway.

"Do you want me to drive you girls?" Jessica's dad called.

"Nah, thanks! We'll walk!" she replied.

As the girls walked and talked, Jessica got the feeling that somebody was following them. She noticed a figure out of the corner of her eye. She'd seen the same coloured t-shirt twice.

"Do you think you could talk non-stop about a topic for a whole minute?" Jessica asked.

"I guess so. Challenge accepted."

"Okay, let's give it a go. Try talking about your favourite food," Jessica prompted her. Jessica held up her watch and tilted it slightly until it was at just the right angle for her to see who was behind them. As Tessa talked about burgers and fries, Jessica adjusted her wrist slightly, checking different angles. That's when she saw the same coloured t-shirt again. It was a guy that looked about fifteen, and he was holding a skateboard as he walked. He had messy, light brown hair down to his shoulders, and he wore glasses with thin black frames. He had a small, black backpack over his shoulder, and there was a helmet strapped to the outside of it. Jessica quickly tilted her wrist away.

"Well done. That was a full minute," Jessica announced.

As the girls walked through the shopping centre's sliding glass doors, Jessica used the reflection of the glass to take another glance behind her. The guy

with the skateboard was still there. She grabbed
Tessa by the arm.

"I know where we can start." She led Tessa up an
escalator and around a corner to the stationery
shop. All the way, she was using every reflective
surface she could to see what the guy was doing. He
followed the girls up the escalator, but hung back
when they entered the shop.

Jessica made sure they took their time inside.
They checked out everything bright, glittery, and
scented. As Jessica held up stationery to show
Tessa, she snuck a glimpse at the guy with the
skateboard. After a few minutes, he moved away.
Jessica was relieved he'd gone, but was freaked out
by him following them. She figured it must have
been to do with her, and it'd be best not to scare
Tessa by telling her. It felt like yet another thing on
top of the lies she'd already told Tessa.

Jessica kept a lookout for the skateboard guy but
didn't see him again.

Later that Saturday afternoon, Jessica was sitting
alone in her room. She was working on her current

piece of art while testing her memory on some new
Japanese words. Her watch buzzed and prompted
her to unlock the screen. She entered the security
code, and a message appeared:

> *Mission this Thursday. Meet at*
> *training centre. Driver will pick you up*
> *at 9:40 p.m. Team departs for mission*
> *at 11 p.m. No practice this Monday.*
>
> *Clint.*

Jessica had been anticipating this moment since
her first training session. She was fearing it, and at
the same time, looking forward to it.

The last few days had flown by for Jessica. She'd
concentrated on her training and found it hard to
focus at school.

Walking home from school on Wednesday, she
noticed somebody following her again. It started
with the, *click-clack, click-clack* of skateboard
wheels rolling along a footpath a fair distance away.
As the noise got closer, it stopped. When she
crossed a side street, she managed to sneak a quick
look behind her, whilst checking for cars. She saw

the same guy that had been following her and Tessa at the shopping centre.

Jessica decided not to go directly home. She didn't want to lead him to where she lived. Jessica walked up a couple of streets until she got to a small reserve with trees and a dirt path. She knew if she was quick enough, she could run a short way, turn a corner, run a little farther, and turn another corner. This would make it difficult for the guy to know where she'd gone. She suddenly ran full speed down the dirt track. She turned left, then left again. After running a little more, she turned right, taking her back onto the main road she'd been on a few minutes ago. She slowed down, but kept running, and concentrated on taking light steps. It was now hard for anyone to hear her, and she was able to listen out for anyone close by. *I think I lost him with all those turns.*

After walking a little more, Jessica felt it was safe to head home.

She sighed with relief when she made it to her front door. But she remained uneasy, still feeling like somebody was watching her.

Chapter 11: First Mission

It was Thursday. It was the night of Jessica's first mission. Her watch buzzed, asking for her code. She read a new message:

Your car is now approaching. Number plate 2AX4EV. Driver's name is Zac.

Jessica had crept out so often, it had become second nature. Her arms and legs moved from memory, taking her equipment from under her bed, grabbing her backpack, and removing the flyscreen.

She was happy to see Zac. "Hey, Zac. How's it going tonight?"

"Good evening, young lady. I'll be your driver again for this evening."

Following a short drive, the sound of gravel crunching under car tyres rang out into the night as Zac drove into the factory carpark.

"Best of luck tonight, young lady."

"Thanks, Zac. Will you be here waiting for me later?" Jessica hadn't been on a real mission yet. She was nervous about how everything would work, including getting home afterward.

"I've been told to wait. Perhaps it's a fairly short mission this time. Sometimes I'm told to come back early the next morning or even several days later. But not this time. This time, I stay here with a blanket and something to read to pass the time. You can relax knowing your ride home will be here waiting for you," Zac reassured her.

"Thanks. That's good to know. See you soon."

Jessica walked into the training room. Her teammates were checking equipment, packing for the mission, and adjusting clothing. Clint walked over and handed her some clothes.

"You can change into these in the rooms out back. Let me know if there's any problem with the sizing." He marched off, his steely eyes darting around the room. He was even more serious than usual.

Over the next half hour, Jessica prepared for the mission. She changed into something similar to a ninja uniform. It was midnight blue, had lots of straps to tighten the material around her body, and had plenty of pockets and a belt. Jessica found places to store her throwing stars, sai, and lock picks. One of the specialist instructors helped her with the weapons. He gave her an extra sai and explained she should carry three and he'd show her how to use the third one soon.

Jessica was eager to talk to Dalmar. She was nervous about the mission and how she was going to make it home before morning. Although Zac thought it would be quick, she wondered how true that could be. *Where will it be, and how simple can it be?*

"Hey, Jessica. Are you feeling okay?" Dalmar asked as he approached her. He was also wearing a midnight blue uniform and had a couple of nunchaku tucked in his belt.

"You know, I'm nervous," Jessica replied.

"It'll be alright. Shortly, Clint will give us a mission briefing. We'll find out details and what each of us need to do. We usually find out the location and how long it's expected to take. Some missions include a lot of waiting, hidden until we can do our thing. Other times, we go straight in." Dalmar put his hand on Jessica's shoulder. "I'm glad you're here. You have great gifts, and I've noticed how well you're using those sai and throwing stars now. It's great to have you on the team."

"Okay, team, gather 'round!" Clint shouted.

Everyone came together in the beanbag area. Clint took a whiteboard marker and started drawing. "We're heading out in a few minutes. It'll take about an hour to get to the target location. It's a local one, so you'll be home before dawn. Our target item is a ruby. It's an amazing, deep red-coloured gem. Gemstones are cut in different ways. This one's a 'Holland rose' cut. Also known as a 'double rose' cut. The shape looks like this." Clint sketched it on the whiteboard. "Its actual size will be about this big." Clint drew a circle on the board.

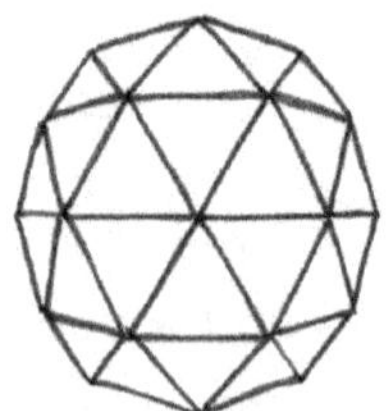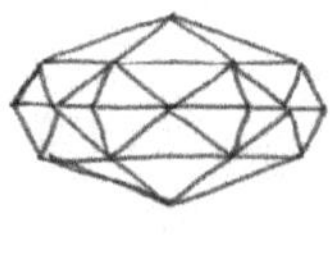

He continued the briefing. "It's being kept in a private collection. That means it's at somebody's house. But don't be fooled. The place is very secure and well-guarded. The guy stole it from an overseas gallery, and they've asked us to get it back. They're embarrassed about losing it. Basically, the gallery displays lots of items like this, but they don't own them. Private owners lend them to the gallery to display, so members of the public can visit and enjoy them. The gallery's meant to keep these things secure. So, it's embarrassing that they let one get stolen. They need us to get this gem back and not involve the police. If the police get involved, the media will find out. They can't afford any negative press. There will be security guards at the front gate to the property and walking around the outer fence. If the owners aren't home, there'll be at least two guards walking around inside the main building where the gem's kept. It's in a secure room, and there's an alarm system and a locked, bullet-proof glass cabinet. We couldn't get many details of what's inside the main building, so we'll need to get straight to that room, do our thing, and back out. There'll be two teams. Team One is Dalmar, Jade, Brooke, and Kai. You'll clear the path for Team Two to take the gem. Team Two is Joseph, Jessica, and

Nikhil. You'll pass the gem to Team One as both teams exit the location. Any questions?" Clint took a deep breath and paused. "Okay, let's go!"

Everyone stepped onto a minibus, and it took off down the street. There was the driver, Clint, a communications specialist named Frank, and all the kids. Frank handed out headsets. Everyone was able to communicate with each other using the devices. Frank had a small desk and computer in front of his seat.

The driver switched off the bus's lights and pulled to the side of the road. The headsets had built-in tracking devices, so Frank was able to see their locations on his computer. He could also see the target location on his screen. He helped the kids walk the last hundred metres to reach the target property's front fence.

Clint spoke through the headsets to the kids. "Team One, you're up."

Brooke swung a grappling hook and threw it to the top of the property's high fence.

One at a time, Dalmar, Jade, Brooke, and Kai used the rope to climb over and drop to the other side. They snuck from tree to tree, moving undetected, closer to the main building. Upon reaching it, Dalmar and Jade circled to the left of what appeared to be a large mansion. Brooke and Kai went right.

Dalmar saw a guard walking through the garden. He tapped Jade on the shoulder and pointed. She ran to the guard.

"What are you doing here?" the guard demanded, his body leaning back and his eyes wide. He grabbed his baton.

"Sleep now!" Jade commanded, as she moved her hand in front of his face. Suddenly the guard collapsed, fast asleep.

Meanwhile, another guard confronted Brooke and Kai. Kai grabbed the guard's wrist and teleported both the guard and himself to Jade. As they appeared in front of her, she quickly raised her hand and commanded, "Sleep now!"

Brooke came running to join the others.

Dalmar led the team to a laundry room window. Kai teleported inside, checked around for alarm sensors, then opened the window. The rest of the team entered the mansion. They drew their weapons, and Brooke guarded the door into the laundry.

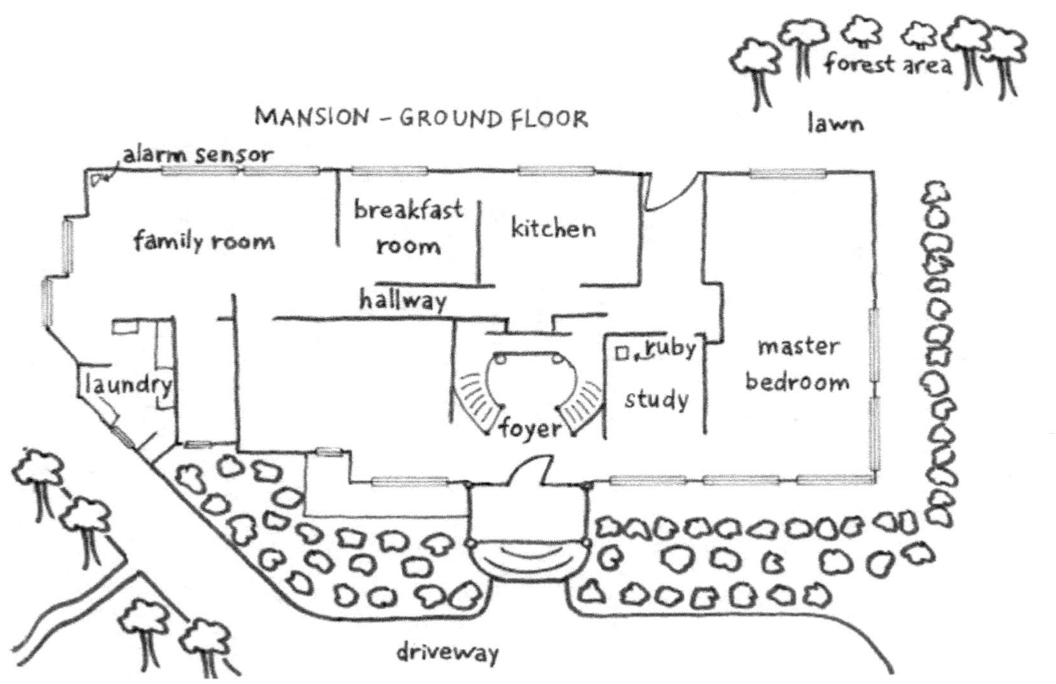

MANSION – GROUND FLOOR
forest area
lawn
alarm sensor
family room
breakfast room
kitchen
hallway
laundry
ruby
study
foyer
master bedroom
driveway

Kai spoke softly into his headset, "Okay, Team Two. You're all clear to join us. Come through the laundry window to the left of the main entrance."

"Copy that," replied Nikhil. "We're on our way."

Team Two used the grappling hook and rope to enter the yard. Nikhil took the lead, followed by Joseph and Jessica. They ran quietly up to the laundry window and established eye contact with Team One before climbing through.

Joseph moved from the laundry into the family room to find an alarm sensor. If he could find one sensor, he'd be able to use it to tap into the system and deactivate the whole thing. He found one on the ceiling in the corner of the room. He motioned for Brooke to join him. She crept up. Using her super-strength, she grabbed hold of Joseph's legs and lifted him effortlessly until he could easily reach the device. Joseph removed the sensor's cover and connected it to his phone with some special leads. He opened an app and used it to deactivate the whole alarm system, also erasing its stored recordings.

"House alarm down and cleared," Joseph whispered into his headset.

Brooke moved back to the laundry to re-join Team One, as Team Two moved through the house in search of the gemstone.

Nikhil, Joseph, and Jessica crept out of the family room and into a hallway. The walls were covered with artwork. Nikhil led them into a foyer. The huge entrance area had a staircase on both sides, leading to the mansion's second level. He was just about to walk through the foyer and into what looked like a study when he heard voices. He quickly raised his arm, alerting Joseph and Jessica.

"Where were they off to tonight?" a man's voices asked.

"I dunno. Some fancy party, I guess. They should be back soon," another man answered.

Nikhil listened carefully. It sounded like the two men were talking at the top of one of the staircases. Then there were footsteps. They were coming downstairs. Nikhil motioned to Joseph.

Using his super-speed, Joseph ran back to the laundry and let Team One know. Jade came along as Joseph returned to Nikhil, creeping through the mansion. Nikhil and Jessica were hiding in the foyer under one of the staircases. Nikhil turned invisible momentarily, then reappeared. "They're both on the left side. Halfway up the stairs. They've stopped, and they're just standing there," he whispered to the others.

Jade rushed into the open part of the foyer and to the bottom of the left staircase.

"Sleep now! Sleep now!" she yelled, looking at one man, then the other. Both men slumped to the ground, sleeping awkwardly on the stairs.

Jade stayed with Team Two as they moved through the foyer and into what looked like a study.

"Jade now with Team Two. Team Two entering study," Nikhil said quietly into his headset.

"Copy that," replied Dalmar.

"Status report of teams. Dalmar, Brooke, and Kai in laundry. Nikhil, Jade, Joseph, and Jessica entering study," Dalmar explained to Clint and Frank.

"Copy that," replied Clint.

The study was a large room with bookcases covering the length of one of the walls. Another wall was covered with precious-looking artefacts from around the world. These included large copper plates, a medieval shield, an ancient-looking spear, axe, and swords. There were also doors leading to two other rooms. One seemed to be a bedroom. The wall facing the front yard was lined with large, fancy-looking windows.

"Psst," Joseph said quietly. As the other kids looked at him, he pointed to one corner of the room. Sitting on a small pedestal, and secured under a thick, clear cover, was a gemstone. They all stepped over to it and crowded around. It was a deep red and shaped in the same way Clint had drawn the gem on the whiteboard.

"We've found it. It's in the study," Nikhil quietly announced through his headset.

They worked quickly. Joseph hacked into the security system that was specifically securing the gem. It was on a separate circuit to the home alarm he'd already deactivated. Within a couple of minutes, he'd deactivated the gem's security.

"Security for gem is down. Good to go," Joseph confirmed. By deactivating the security, the bulletproof casing covering the gem unlocked and could be lifted off. Jessica used her powers to carefully lift the cover up and across, setting it down on the ground. She then lifted the gem up and away from where it sat. Although the security seemed to have been deactivated, it was safer for Jessica to use her mind to move the gem than to have anyone touch it yet. She moved it in front of Nikhil. He took a small felt pouch from his pocket, grabbed the gem, and put it in.

"I'll go invisible as soon as we're out of the mansion and reappear when we're on the minibus," Nikhil informed the team.

"We've secured the gem. I repeat, we've secured the gem. Prepare for exit," Joseph relayed through his headset.

"Heads up. I'll be setting guards to wake as we exit," Jade warned.

"Team One exiting now. Clearing the path," Dalmar said as he, Brooke, and Kai climbed out the laundry window. They started making their way across the front lawn to the fence.

"Copy that. We're right behind you. Coming out of the study now," Nikhil replied.

Jade moved across the foyer and up the staircase to where she'd left the two guards sleeping.

"Shortly, you will wake up," she instructed them. "You will not remember anything from today." She clicked her fingers.

"One minute until staircase guards wake up," Jade warned the others via her headset. She moved down the hallway, into the laundry, and paused there for the others to follow.

Just then, there was a flash of light and a huge bang. Nikhil, Joseph, and Jessica were caught in the doorway between the study and the foyer. The sound of shattering glass filled the study. Its widows facing the front yard blew apart. More breaking glass could be heard from the room next to the study. Shadowy figures wearing black clothing stormed through the study windows as the room filled up with strange-coloured smoke. More figures stormed in from the other room.

Joseph used his powers, moving like lightning. He stumbled for a moment, then knocked down several of the intruders. He darted across the foyer, down the hallway, and into the laundry.

Nikhil turned invisible. He held the gem tightly as he weaved through the intruders. He bumped into the walls as he ran along the hallway, feeling like a pinball. The coloured smoke everywhere made it hard to see. He managed to meet the others in the laundry.

"Exit. Go, go, go!" Nikhil yelled into the headset. There were figures dashing down the hallway after them. Out into the night, the three ran.

"Jessica!" Nikhil yelled into his headset, panting for air as he ran across the lawn. There was no response. He tried again. "Jessica, copy?!"

In the confusion of shattering glass, stun grenades, smoke bombs, and four intruders storming the mansion, Jessica had become disoriented. She found herself in the master bedroom. It was the large room off from the study. There was broken glass and empty smoking canisters on the floor. She crouched in the corner, trying to get her bearings.

Two shadowy figures had rushed down the hallway. The other two were in the foyer, watching the guards on the staircase waking up.

"These two are just guards," said one of them.

"Damn it! Leave them. Let's check the study," replied the other.

Jessica jumped up and dived out the bedroom's smashed windows and into the cool night air. She ran as fast as she could along the side wall of the mansion. Unfortunately, she was heading away from the front fence. She was running towards the back of the property. There was a lawn and about ten metres past that, a lot of trees. It looked like a small forest of young pines.

"Somebody's gone out this window!" one of the figures yelled to the other.

"Bedroom clear!" the other yelled in reply.

They both pursued Jessica, out through the smashed window and around the side of the mansion.

"Did you see where they went?" one asked.

"I think …" the other trailed off. He saw some movement between the pine trees. Although it was dark and at a distance, the intruder recognised Jessica as she ducked down in the forest, trying to keep herself quiet as her body gasped for air.

The intruder that saw her spoke to the other one. "Let's split up and find them. I'll check the trees over there. You check the side and around the front of the building."

"Okay. Yell out if you find anything."

Jessica watched as a lone figure approached the treed area. She silently drew her sai. Each hand gripped the handles nervously. She was now confident training with these weapons, but using them to hurt somebody was something she'd never considered. Jessica's mind was racing. *This is nothing like a training session. Am I meant to jump out and fight this person? Or only use my sai to defend myself as a last resort?*

"Jessica!" the figure said in a loud whisper as he got closer. "I know it's you. It's okay."

Jessica remained very still. She wasn't sure if this guy could see her or was just guessing she was there. *How does he know my name?*

"Jessica!" the guy said again. "We don't have much time."

Jessica recognised the voice. But she couldn't believe what she was hearing. It seemed impossible. She angled the sai forward, ready to strike if needed. She tightened her grip on the handles even more.

"It's me. Karim," he said, as he slowly raised his empty hands. "I just want to talk, but we don't have much time."

Jessica carefully turned off her headset. "Okay," she agreed. She still couldn't believe what was happening.

Karim cautiously approached, keeping enough distance so she couldn't strike him in a panic. He squatted down and motioned for Jessica to do the same.

"We were on a mission to stop you. We were told your team would be breaking into this building. We were assigned to protect the ruby," Karim explained.

"Who do you work for?" asked Jessica.

"I don't know. And I've been wondering if I'm working for the good side or the bad side. Some of the assignments we do ... I just can't see how they could be good. I've been seeing too many things that make me question everything," Karim admitted.

"What kind of things?"

"Well, I don't see them directly. I see other people's memories. That's my thing. It's what I do. I can access other people's memories if I'm near them. I've pieced together some ideas on what's happening by reading the memories of my teammates and bosses. But it's hard. I can't just read every single memory. I get pieces of things. I get feelings and images from people's minds. I can't choose what I get," Karim said.

"So, you knew I had special powers? You could see my memories of when I'd used them?"

"Yes. Your ability to move things with your mind. How you've kept that a secret. How you've learned to use sai, learned to pick locks, learned to speak Japanese," Karim continued.

"Who else is on your team? Do they all have powers? Can you quit any time, or are you stuck?" Jessica questioned.

"We don't have time now to talk about it. Let's talk tomorrow, after school," Karim replied.

"Sorry, I can't. I work at the Mr. Watson's barber shop on Friday afternoons. How about Saturday morning?"

"Yeah, okay. But why don't we just talk at school?" Karim asked.

"Probably not safe. What if somebody overhears us? They'll either freak out or think we're crazy."

"We can meet at the park at the top of High Street?" Karim asked.

"Sure. See you there. Saturday morning at ten."

Karim left Jessica and ran to his teammate, who was now coming towards the forest area, searching for him.

"Any luck finding them?" asked Karim.

"Nah. They must have gotten away. Let's go find the others," Karim's teammate replied.

Karim made sure they moved away, providing a clear path for Jessica. She ran down the side of the mansion to the front fence.

She was near the top corner of the property, a long way from where the others had already scaled the fence. Everyone else was now in the minibus. She switched her headset back on.

"I'm at the top corner of the property. I'm at the fence now. Anyone copy?" Jessica said in a panic.

"Copy that," Frank responded. "We're coming to get you. You went off air for a while. Your headset and tracker were offline. We could see from the tracker that you headed to the back of the property, but we didn't know what was going on after that."

Within a few seconds, Joseph was on the other side of the fence. He swung the grappling hook, and it clawed onto the top of the fence. He used it to drop down next to her, bringing the rope with him. They both climbed to safety.

"Come on! This way!" he yelled.

She followed him up the road and saw the minibus waiting with its engine running. The two kids climbed in, and the bus took off.

They arrived back at the training centre. They were tired, but still buzzing with adrenaline.

"Okay, gather 'round team!" Clint instructed.

The team moved to the beanbag area. After most missions, Clint would debrief with the team. He'd talk through what went well, what could have been better, and anything anyone was confused about.

"Who were those others that stormed the mansion?" Nikhil asked immediately.

Brooke jumped in to respond. "Remember a few missions back we came across that other team? They seemed to be there for the same reason we were. At least a couple of them had special gifts. It was at that art gallery in Milan, I think …. Perhaps those guys from tonight are connected?"

"What happened to you, Jessica? Did you get to see any of those others when they were trying to hunt you down?" Joseph asked.

Jessica cleared her throat. "I got confused with all the smoke and noise. There seemed to be so many intruders. They broke windows in the study and the bedroom. Maybe the foyer too. There were bright flashes of light and loud noises. There was coloured smoke. I couldn't balance properly. I couldn't see where I was going. I got out the bedroom window and ran for it. A couple of them tried to find me, but they gave up. Then I ran to the bus."

Jessica tried hard to keep her mind blank so Dalmar wouldn't find out what actually happened. She glanced over at him. He was looking at her a little strangely, but then looked away.

Clint spoke up. "Okay. That other team used stun and smoke grenades tonight. We haven't done any training with either of those weapons. But we did cover them in some information sessions a while back. Anyone joining us recently may not know about them. Stun grenades create bright flashes and loud noises. They're used to stun, to disorient, to knock people off balance. Smoke grenades or smoke bombs are used to fill an area with smoke. It makes it hard to see and disorients people." Clint looked to the ground and slowly ran his hand up and down his jaw, then looked up again. "Alright, we just need to be cautious. We'll arrange some new headsets that record video, so if people storm in on us again, we'll have some footage. I'll make sure they continuously record and work well …. We don't want any more problems like tonight with headsets switching off." He looked at Jessica as he finished his sentence. She sheepishly nodded in agreement.

"Did we get a bonus for tonight's mission because we got the ruby?" Kai piped up, changing the topic, much to Jessica's relief.

"Yes. Tonight was worth four thousand five hundred each. That includes the bonus," Clint confirmed. "Well done again. Go get some rest. See you for training on Monday."

With that, everyone gathered their bags and left the training centre. As they walked out, they saw their drivers waiting. Jessica was glad to see Zac and couldn't wait to get home to sleep.

Chapter 12: Searching for Answers

Jessica's Friday had been reasonably uneventful. She enjoyed working at Mr. Watson's in the afternoon. She'd missed listening in on the interesting conversations he had with customers. She was glad to hear his new assistants were doing well. It sounded like they may even want to keep working there, so Mr. Watson wouldn't have to find anyone more permanent.

Mr. Watson switched off the lights and opened the door for Jessica. He then locked up for the day.

"Oh, it looks like your friend's here to meet you again," he said, looking towards Dalmar, who was sitting on the bench two shops down.

"How did you know he was my friend?" Jessica asked suspiciously.

"I remember him meeting you here one Saturday."

"Wow. You notice a lot of stuff. I'd better go say hello. See you next Friday!"

She approached Dalmar. "Hey. What are you doing here?"

"I wanted to let you know something about last night," Dalmar said. "I didn't want to say it with the whole team around. It could have freaked the others out. I don't think they realise those guys that blasted in had any powers. But when you went offline, we were worried. Brooke and I tried to look for you. We got over the fence and halfway across the front lawn. Then it was like we hit a wall. There wasn't anything there. We couldn't see anything. We just couldn't go any farther. It was some weird forcefield. We saw one of those guys at the front door holding his hands up towards us. It was really weird …. They definitely have powers. I know it for sure."

"Geez! This is getting crazy. Before I met you, I didn't even know anyone else had powers. I kept mine such a secret. Only my brother and the barber knew. My parents don't even know. I was so embarrassed of what I could do. I felt like something was wrong with me. Now I'm in a team full of kids with powers. Powers are seen as something to be grateful for, not embarrassed of. We go on dangerous missions where other teams turn up and attack us. And they have powers! You mentioned it happened once before. But you never saw those ones use their powers, yeah? It was just that guy on your team who said they had them? Seems he was right. On top of this, somebody's been following me. This is totally insane. We can't even get out of this craziness because we're not allowed to leave the team," Jessica rambled.

Dalmar really didn't have anything else to share with Jessica. She wondered if he just wanted to tell somebody about what had happened to him and Brooke. Or if it was something more devious.

When talking to Dalmar this time, Jessica noticed something weird. She thought she could actually tell he was trying to read her mind. In the past, she only knew he was because he'd respond to what she was thinking. But this time was different. She could sense something. It was like a pebble being thrown into a pond and creating ripples. It was weird, but she could sense these ripples from her head to

Dalmar's. Almost like they were carrying her thoughts to him.

Later that night, Jessica was working on a new manga drawing while practicing her Japanese vocabulary. She let her mind wander to the conversation she'd had with Dalmar earlier that day. *I need to find out more about this team I'm in. I wonder if Dalmar thinks it's all as crazy as I do? Perhaps not. He's been part of it for much longer than I have. He lied to me when he first met me. He was playing his part for Clint. This afternoon, did he want to see if I held any info back at the debrief? Did Clint put him up to it? Did he only tell me about those other guys with powers to see if I'd tell him about Karim? Can I trust him? If I don't trust him, then how do I stop him from finding out about Karim? How do I stop him from reading my mind?*

Jessica sat a little straighter in her chair and cleared her papers and pens to one side. She grabbed her phone and began to research. She searched for anything she could find that might help her understand the team she was in.

Jessica typed into the search bar: *Milan, Italy, art gallery robbery heist theft.*

She looked through the results. No luck. She tried a few more searches.

Dalmar mind read psychic powers.

Recover stolen gems contact Clint.

No luck. She then unlocked her watch and scrolled through old messages. She went back to the search bar and entered: *Vehicle registration number plate 2AX4EV.*

Nothing useful came up. Only a whole lot of links for buying new and used cars. After pausing for a moment, she typed: *large Holland rose double rose cut ruby.*

There were quite a few images of rubies similar to the one from the mansion. She added a word and searched again.

Gallery large Holland rose double rose cut ruby.

Interestingly, there were no galleries claiming to have that shape of ruby on display, or in their collection. There were plenty of listings for other shaped rubies and other gems cut in the Holland rose style. *If there was a huge ruby somewhere in an art gallery, it would show up somewhere on these lists. Even if it weren't currently on display. These lists do include items that are, "not publicly displayed at this time." Does this mean Clint was lying about the ruby coming from a gallery? Does the team simply believe Clint's stories, never checking to see if they're true? Maybe the truth doesn't matter. Everyone's stuck in the team and can't leave anyway.*

Chapter 13: Karim

Suddenly, Jessica awoke. She panicked. She was running late for her Saturday morning shift at Mr. Watson's. Then she remembered she only worked on Friday afternoons. She sighed and lay in bed for a few more minutes.

The whole family sat at the table eating breakfast. Jessica was so happy. It wasn't often her mum felt well enough to eat at the same time as the rest of them.

"I have some very exciting news to share," their dad announced. "I had a random call out of the blue from a recruiter earlier this week. He must have gotten my resume some time over the last year. Goodness knows, I've sent it to so many employers, recruiters, and job agents. Anyway, he said he had a job he thought was perfect for me."

"That's wonderful!" Jessica exclaimed, her eyes lighting up.

"Nice one, Dad!" Tim added.

"Your dad's tried so hard to balance things over the last couple of years. It really feels like this could be the point where our luck changes," their mum said, her eyes twinkling with hope.

"It gets better," their dad continued. "I met the company for an interview and heard back today that I've got the job! I start Monday. The hours and flexibility fit in with caring for Mum. It's like a miracle … too good to be true. But if it's a miracle, I'll take it. Things may finally start becoming good around here, J-Bear, T-man."

Jessica was extremely happy for her dad. All of a sudden, his luck had changed. It was what the whole family had been hoping for so desperately.

Before Jessica left the house to meet Karim, her dad stopped her at the door. "With the money from my new job starting to come in soon, you'll be able to keep what you earn from selling your artwork. You'll finally be able to spend some money on yourself. You must hate having to wear those old clothes. You never complain about it, and I'm so grateful for that," her dad said.

"Thanks, Dad. I just sold another drawing," she lied. "I'll add a bit more money to the jar before we stop using it. That'll cover things until your first payday."

"Jessica! Over here!" Karim called. He was sitting under a large tree in the park, waiting for her.

"Hey, Karim," Jessica greeted, as she sat down beside him.

"I can't believe what happened the other night," he said. "It feels more like a dream than reality."

"I know what you mean. I can't believe Lawson Primary has two of us running around in these teams. Have you found any others at school?"

"Nope. Just you," Karim replied.

"Well, I'm already wanting to retire." Jessica laughed awkwardly. "I liked the sound of the money to start with. My family's been having a tough time for a while, with Mum being sick. But now it just seems I'm stuck in a crazy team on dangerous missions … and I don't even know if I'm working for the good guys or bad guys."

"I know exactly what you mean. Your story sounds like mine. I'm glad it's not just me. It's good to be able to talk to somebody else about this stuff," Karim said.

"Hey, do you know anything about that ruby everyone was trying to get? Our boss said it was stolen from a gallery. We were taking it back. But I couldn't find anything online to confirm that," Jessica explained.

"Like I mentioned on the night I met you, we were told a team was going to try and steal it from the owner's mansion. We were told which night it was planned and asked to help keep it safe," Karim replied.

"Somebody in your team knows what our team is doing. Otherwise, how would your team know the exact date?"

"A double-agent perhaps? Somebody working for both teams?" Karim suggested.

"Another reason I just want to be able to get out of this crazy mess."

As Jessica and Karim chatted, Tessa walked up High Street. She was meeting Jessica in the afternoon, so had come to buy a few things in the morning. As if on autopilot, Tessa took a detour via the barber shop to wave hello through the window. She'd forgotten Jessica no longer worked Saturday mornings. When she couldn't see Jessica in the shop, she turned to walk home. She caught sight of Jessica chatting with Karim. She went to run over to the park, but stopped. She remembered the way Karim had looked at Jessica at school and figured she'd leave them to keep talking and find out all about it when she met her later.

"You know, I've always wanted to talk to you more, but I was too shy," Karim admitted.

Jessica's eyes widened. "Really? Why? We talk sometimes. Like the time we did that science project across classes. You were in my group."

"Not like that though. Talking like this. Talking about things outside of school …. Reading people's memories can be lonely. It's hard when I know a lot about people and I haven't talked to them much. I don't know how to pretend I don't know much about them. I find it's easier to be the quiet one in the corner," Karim explained, visibly upset by his situation.

"Well, make sure you talk to me whenever you want to," Jessica encouraged, hoping to cheer him up.

"Thanks, Jessica," Karim replied. "We should let each other know what's going on in our teams too. It might help us piece everything together."

Jessica hesitated for a moment, weighing whether she should fully trust Karim yet. "Actually, can I ask you about your powers? When you read somebody's memories, how does it feel? Does it feel a certain way when you're actually reading them?"

"How do you mean? Like when I'm actually sitting there doing it?"

"Yeah. Does it feel like you're connected to the person? Does it feel like their thoughts are all around you and you're grabbing at them? Does it feel like waves or ripples that are coming towards you?" Jessica asked.

"Probably waves or ripples. It feels like a connection between them and me. As I get their memories in my mind, it does feel a bit like waves between us. Why's that?" Karim asked, curious at Jessica's questions.

"Can you try to read my memories now? I want to see if it feels like waves to me when you do it."

"Okay," Karim said.

Jessica got the same feeling she had when Dalmar had been reading her mind. It felt like ripples in a pond, from her mind to his. Jessica had an idea. She concentrated on the waves. She then started to apply the same power to them that she would apply to move an object. She imagined the waves then being drawn back towards her. This was how she'd usually make things move. She'd concentrate on the object and where she wanted it to go. This time, instead of an object, she was concentrating on her mind waves. She focused on stopping the waves from going towards Karim's head, and drawing them back towards her own.

"Hey!" Karim exclaimed. He looked puzzled. "What did you do?"

"Sorry. I was just seeing if I could block you," Jessica said.

"Yeah, it worked. I was reading you, and then it felt like something was pulling my mind. It was kind of like I was a fish on a hook. Then my brain when fuzzy, and I lost focus. Where I'd usually see your memories, kind of like a movie playing, it went dark."

"Wow. I can use my powers to shift mind waves. That's intense. I thought I could only shift real objects … but I can move brain waves around. Must be all the practice I've been doing. It's strengthened my powers," Jessica said with surprise. She realised she'd said it out loud and regretted it for a moment. But Karim did seem very trustworthy. She hoped he was now that he knew more about the extent of her powers than anyone else.

"That's handy," Karim said. "And very, very cool." He smiled at her.

Jessica tried for a moment to draw Karim's thoughts towards her brain. She felt like she was moving the waves towards her. But she couldn't read them, so they just felt like waves lapping against the side of a ship. Her newly discovered power was only good in preventing others from reading her mind. It wouldn't help her read anyone else's.

"Hello, Jessica," Tessa's mum greeted her as she came into the house. "Tessa's upstairs in her room."

"Thanks," Jessica replied.

Tessa was playing games on her phone and looked up as Jessica entered the room.

"I've almost cracked level eight of Spells Master," Tessa shrieked.

"Awesome. Can I have a look?" Jessica sat down next to Tessa on her bed.

The girls leant in towards the screen as Tessa continued to play.

"Anything interesting been happening?" Tessa asked.

"Nah, not really. Dad got a job though, so that's good. It'll help with things getting back to normal, as much as they can, while Mum's still sick."

"Any boy news? That guy from the other school? Or anyone from our school?" Tessa probed.

"Nah. Nothing really," Jessica replied.

"Are you holding out on me? I went past the barber shop to wave hello. I forgot you don't work Saturdays anymore. I saw you and Karim talking in the park," Tessa said.

"Oh, yeah," Jessica admitted. "I was in the park, and he was there. We talked for a bit. You know, he told me he wanted to talk to me more at school, but was too shy. But he just wanted to be friendly. Maybe that's why he was looking at me that day. Anyway, it was a nice chat. I should have mentioned it to you. I didn't think about it."

"That's okay. You know how I like to keep up with any news of your love life," Tessa teased.

"Haha. Yep." Jessica was feeling so bad, lying to her best friend again.

Chapter 14: Lightning Kid

"Good evening, young lady." Zac twisted his head around from the driver's seat to welcome Jessica into the car.

"Hi, Zac."

That night at training, Jessica wanted to see if she could use her power to stop Dalmar from reading her mind. If she and Karim were going to work together on anything, she needed to make sure Dalmar didn't find out. She thought Dalmar seemed cool but not necessarily interested in doing anything that'd upset Clint or the team.

Jessica got her chance at the end of the night.

"Hey, Jessica," Dalmar said. He came up to her, nodding his head. "That was a full-on training session. I was hoping we'd have a break, but it was pure weapons training. I saw you over there with your sai. Looking sharp!" he complimented her.

"Thanks. You too."

As they chatted, Jessica concentrated on picking up the mind waves. She could feel them rippling towards Dalmar. She could feel him reading her mind.

"Are you trying to work out if I'm reading your mind?" Dalmar asked her.

"Haha. Yeah," she replied.

Jessica experimented with a thought. *Dalmar, you're an idiot*. She quickly used her power to pull the thought back and hold it from him. She tried again. *Quick! Look behind you!* She pulled her thought back again. Dalmar didn't react. He didn't look behind himself. He just kept talking about the training session. *Yes! It works!*

Dalmar paused mid-sentence. "What works?" he asked.

"Oh, nothing. I was just thinking about a new technique with my sai," Jessica lied. "Sorry. What were you saying?"

★ ★ ★

For the next three days, Jessica went home via the bank's ATM. She withdrew five hundred dollars each afternoon, adding it to the jar in the kitchen. She wanted to make sure her dad had enough to keep paying the bills while he waited for his first payday.

★ ★ ★

Jessica felt good it was Friday morning. But the feeling was short-lived. As soon as she walked through the school gate, the bullies were at her. Greg, Chloe, and Tien walked up to her.

"Hey, Poor Poor," Greg teased.

"Poory-Poory-Poor-Poor," Tien added, giggling. She wasn't always a bully, but whenever she was with Greg and Chloe, she'd join in.

Jessica did her best to ignore them as she walked past.

Later that morning, Jessica saw Tien sitting on her own at recess. She approached her.

"Does calling me names make you feel better about yourself?" Jessica asked. Tien looked at her without saying anything. "Are you so rich you think you could never end up poor? If your parents got sick, do you think you'd just keep cruising through life without anything changing?" Jessica continued.

Tien was in shock. She shook her head slightly. Jessica walked off. *Wow! I can't believe I actually said something to her. I've been wanting to confront her for so long. Catching her alone really worked. She had nothing smart to say back.*

"Top of the afternoon to you, Jess!" Mr. Watson greeted as she walked into the shop.

"Hey, Mr. Watson," Jessica replied. She went out back to grab a dust pan and brush. Being in the shop felt like home to her. There was a light scent of hair cream and the familiar sound of scissors snipping away, as Mr. Watson cut someone's hair. Something was different today, though. Most days in the past, Jessica would enter the shop and feel a sense of relief. She'd feel relief from the bullies and what they'd said to her that day. But it was different today. As she entered the shop, it didn't feel like she was sheltering from a storm. Having confronted

Tien, she felt empowered. She knew Greg and Chloe would be trickier to deal with, but she was ready.

"It's almost that time again, Jess," Mr. Watson said, as he switched off the cash register and grabbed his coat. "You know, it's working out well with my grandchildren. They've enjoyed it here. In fact, they're now happy to work on Fridays too. You don't have to worry about working next week."

"Oh," Jessica replied. As much as she wanted Friday afternoons to do other stuff, she'd miss the shop.

He sensed her apprehension. "Unless you still want to work Fridays?" he asked. "Is the artwork business still running hot? Or do you still need a little cash to get through?"

"No, it's going well. I'll miss this," she said.

"Never mind. You're always welcome to drop in for a visit, any time. And if you ever need some extra pocket change, you can let me know," Mr. Watson said with a kind smile.

"Thank you so much! I'll be sure to say hello when I'm walking past."

"Say hi to the family for me, Jess." Mr. Watson switched off the lights and followed Jessica out the door.

Jessica ran across the street to the ATM. She was excited to be finally drawing out some money she could spend on herself.

She put the cash in her purse and tucked it deep into a pocket. She started walking down the street towards home. She had a strange feeling she was being followed, so she walked a little quicker. Some footsteps behind her started walking quicker too. She was coming up to the drycleaners. In between that shop and the newsagency was a narrow alleyway. Jessica made a snap decision to run down it. As soon as she was at the corner of the dry-cleaning shop, she stepped to the left, into the alley. She ran a few steps and ducked down behind a large industrial bin. It was one of those bins about the size of a small car. She stayed very quiet and listened. She heard some footsteps stop, then start again. They were coming towards her.

"I know you're there," she heard a voice say. "You have to come out. There's nowhere to run."

The voice sounded very young. She didn't recognise it. Jessica decided to come out to see who it was. After all, he definitely knew she was hiding somewhere nearby. As she stepped out from behind the bin, hoping to see a friendly face, she was totally surprised. In front of her, about ten steps away, stood a boy. He looked no older than her. He even looked a couple of years younger. He took a few steps forward. She noticed his hands. It looked like there was lightning dancing around between his fingers. He raised them up towards her. Jessica grabbed at her waist, where she wore her sai during training. But of course, they weren't there. She saw little forks of electricity jumping from one of the boy's hands to the other.

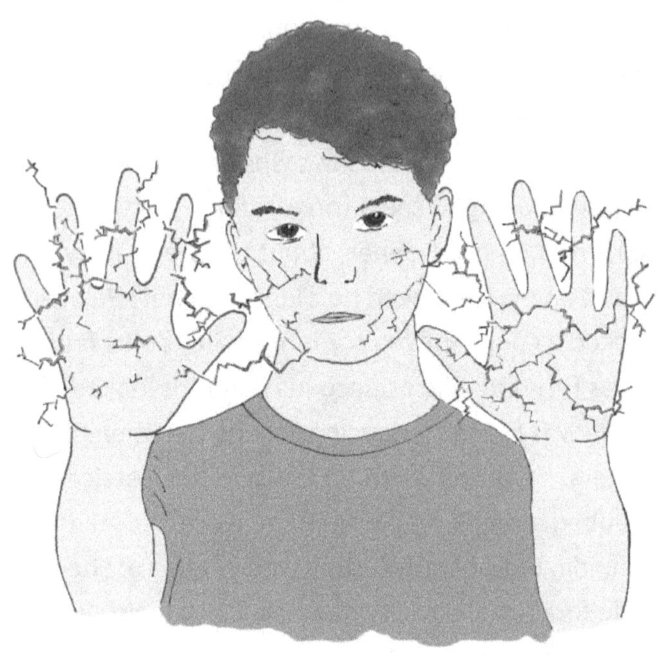

Jessica thought of ways to stall the kid. She thought of questions to ask him so she could use the time to work out her escape. It would be really difficult if his electricity was strong and could reach to the end of the alley. She stared at him and thought.

Just then, she heard a *click clack, click clack* of skateboard wheels rolling along the High Street's footpath. It stopped, and the guy she'd seen several times before appeared in the alley. He lowered his head and took a deep breath. He was holding his board with his left hand, and clenched his right fist beside his body. Slowly, he raised his fist. Jessica watched as he stretched his arm out in the direction of the lightning kid. She noticed the lightning disappear from the kid's hands. The kid looked confused. He narrowed his eyes, and determination spread across his face. Then his face went blank.

"Get lost!" the skateboard guy said to the lightning kid. The lightning kid turned and ran.

"You're okay now, Jessica," the skateboard guy said.

"What? How do you know who I am? Why have you been following me?" Jessica asked.

The guy quickly checked behind him, then approached her. He turned his body so he could talk, whilst checking to see if anyone was coming.

"I'm Chad. I'm a friend of Karim's. He asked me to look out for you. I didn't want to freak you out by following you everywhere, so I just hung around at times when I thought the others were going to try something," Chad explained.

"Well, you did freak me out at the shopping centre."

"Sorry about that. Anyway, that kid with the electric hands … I don't know who he works for, but I've seen him a couple of times before. I think he gets involved recruiting new people. You'll have to be careful," Chad warned.

"This is crazy. I don't know who to trust. I don't know who's out there and what powers they have. I don't even know what they want from me."

"It's okay," Chad assured her. "It happens to most of us. We fly under the radar with our powers. Then we get spotted and recruited into a team. Then we're on everyone's radar. There are spies and double-agents working across all teams. All teams either try to recruit you or take your powers away. Then they give up, and you stay on your original team … feeling stuck and dreaming of wanting to leave. But of course, there's safety in being part of the team, and the money's good too."

"Are you also wanting to leave your team?" Jessica asked Chad.

"Yeah. I'm too used to the money though. And I figure if I left, I'd just be forced to join some other team anyway. Hey, I'll still try and use what Karim and I find out here and there to help you out. I'll follow you occasionally when I've heard the recruiters might be trying to approach you. Home life's pretty tough, so I'm happy to find reasons to stay out and about on my skateboard."

"Thanks, Chad. I don't think I said thanks for helping me with electricity kid. And thanks for helping look out for me. If I had my sai and throwing stars with me all the time, it'd be easier. But I can't carry them around all day."

"No problems. I look out for a few people. I feel it's a way I can use my powers for good and help others stay safe. I'd better get going. See you around." Chad dropped his board in front of him and jumped on it.

Chapter 15: Quick Exit

Jessica awoke to the sound of the vacuum cleaner. She yawned and walked to the kitchen. Her dad was busily tidying up. Tim was already halfway through his breakfast.

"Please tidy up your things this morning, kids. My boss is coming over to drop some papers off that I need to read before Monday. I don't want him seeing a complete mess when I open the door," their dad instructed.

There was a knock at the door. "Can somebody get that?" their dad yelled. "I'll be there in a minute!"

Jessica opened the door. She couldn't believe her eyes.

"Hello. Is your dad here? I have some documents for him," Clint said. He stared straight at Jessica but talked to her as if she were a total stranger. It was like he'd never met her before. He didn't have a knowing look or any indication that he knew who she was. It didn't even seem like he was pretending only for the sake of others in the house. Jessica didn't know how to react. *Do I pretend I've never met him? That's what he's doing.*

"Okay, I'll just get him for you," she replied, trying hard to maintain a blank expression. She hurried away to find her dad and bring him to the door as quickly as possible.

"Ah, hello, Clive," her dad greeted Clint. "I see you've already met my daughter, Jessica."

"Yes, how are you, Jessica?" Clint asked.

"Good thanks, Clive," she responded. *Clive? Why did Dad call him Clive? This is so strange!*

"Anyway, I won't keep you. It's a Saturday morning, after all. I just wanted to drop these off for you before Monday." Clint handed several folders to Jessica's dad.

"Thanks again, Clive. I'll see you bright and early Monday."

"Looking forward to it," Clint replied. "And nice to meet you, Jessica." Clint turned and left.

This can't be pure coincidence. How did Dad suddenly get a job where his boss turns out to be the coach of a secret team I'm in? Even if it was some crazy coincidence, that doesn't explain why Clint's also known as Clive. Is Clint doing this to make sure I can't leave the team? If I leave, does Dad lose his job?

"He's a nice guy, isn't he?" Jessica's dad said after shutting the door.

"I guess. You never mentioned what kind of job it is. Is it doing the same stuff you did at your last job?"

"Spot on. Still working with accounts. You know, all those numbers and spreadsheets I love."

"Sounds boring as ever, Dad." She was happy for him, but very concerned now she knew Clint was involved.

Jessica tried to forget about the morning as she arrived at the shopping centre with Tessa. This was going to be her first time shopping for clothes in what seemed like forever.

"I'm so excited for you." Tessa beamed.

The girls spent the next hour going from shop to shop. Jessica bought news clothes, shoes, and accessories. She even found a couple of things for Tim.

While Tessa tried on some jewellery, Jessica noticed Chad standing a short distance away. He was holding his skateboard in one hand and motioning for Jessica to come over with the other.

"Hey, Tessa. I'll just be a minute. I need to go and talk to someone," Jessica said. Tessa seemed content to continue trying on accessories.

Jessica walked up to Chad. "Hey. What are you doing here? Looking out for me again?" she asked, half joking.

"Yes. And you need to leave now. Seems like the other team's almost given up on recruiting you, but not quite." Chad had a sound of urgency in his voice.

"Okay, what do I need to do?"

"Take your friend and leave using the side entrance. You know, the one that takes you to Crane Street. That should work. If there's any problem, I'll be following them, so don't worry. Now, go."

"Thanks, Chad. Thanks for helping me." Jessica rushed back to Tessa, who'd just decided she didn't want to buy anything.

"Who was that guy you were talking to? He looks a lot older than us? How do you know him?" Tessa fired questions at Jessica.

"We have to go. Come on. Follow me," Jessica said hurriedly. She didn't even have time to come up with a story about who Chad was or why they were now rushing to leave the shopping centre.

"What's this all about?" Tessa asked, short of breath, as they rushed to exit the building.

"I can't explain it now. It's complicated."

"Hey! We tell each other everything. That's our thing. Who was that guy?"

"Tessa, I just can't go into it. There's some stuff happening I can't talk about. Please just go with it for now," Jessica pleaded.

Tessa didn't answer. Her eyes narrowed. She took a deep breath. As she walked next to Jessica, her shoes hit the pavement harder than before.

The girls didn't say much to each other as they walked the rest of the way to Tessa's house. When they got to the front door, Tessa was quite abrupt.

"I have to do some things for my mum. I'll see you some time at school Monday."

"Oh, okay," Jessica replied. She knew Tessa was angry at her. She went along with it and figured it was best to give Tessa some time to cool off. Jessica couldn't explain everything to Tessa. Without sharing the whole story, it'd be too hard to explain about Chad. She totally trusted Tessa. She was just concerned that if Tessa knew, it may put her in danger or make things more difficult. Before Jessica could say anything else, Tessa had gone inside and shut the door.

Jessica walked home. She almost turned around twice, back to Tessa's to tell her everything. It tore

her up inside having her best friend angry at her. It
made her stomach churn. She felt so upset, she
wanted to get home straight away and bury her
head in her pillow and cry.

Chapter 16: Greg's Accident

Greg and Chloe called to Jessica as she walked through the school gate.

"Scram, poverty-girl!" Greg called.

Chloe paused for a moment, noticing Jessica's new pants and shoes.

"Yeah, scram," she added, half-heartedly. She'd expected to be able to pick on Jessica's clothes, but had to rethink when she saw they were new.

Tien was with Greg and Chloe but didn't say anything. She looked uncomfortable and tilted her head down when Greg and Chloe were calling to Jessica.

Jessica did her best to keep walking, but the bullying ruined her Monday morning.

★ ★ ★

"Quick! Quick!" one kid yelled out.

"He's about to fall!" another screamed.

"Hurry!" a third joined in.

Everyone was rushing to see what was happening.

Jessica threw her apple core in the bin and followed the crowd. It was lunchtime, and the schoolyard was full of students. Many of them were now rushing to the stadium where Greg was hanging onto the roof gutter.

"What happened?" somebody asked.

"He went up to get a ball off the roof. He slipped," another replied.

"How stupid. Why would someone do that? The maintenance man clears the roof every couple of weeks," the first kid added.

The stadium roof was high off the ground. Greg's feet were dangling as he held the roof's guttering. If he fell, it'd be at least a two-storey drop. Jessica moved to the front of the crowd. There were two teachers yelling frantically into their phones.

Another had run off to get a ladder. But it didn't look like Greg could hold on much longer. His left hand kept slipping. His fingers were tired. His right arm was straining under the added weight. His right hand was clawing at the gutter, desperately holding on.

Chloe was almost directly under Greg. She looked up at him. "Hold on! Hold on!" she called. She then swung around to the crowd ferociously. Like a wild animal, she screamed, "Somebody do something!"

Now both of Greg's hands were slipping, shaking and moving a lot. He couldn't hold on much longer. He was trying to get a proper grip. Every time he tried, his legs swung in the air. It made it harder for him to keep hold. His chest was moving rapidly. His breathing was frantic. His left hand totally lost its grip. He was about to drop.

Jessica jumped forward, pushing Chloe out of the way. She positioned herself directly under Greg, just as his right hand gave up. His body fell fast. In that split second, Jessica concentrated like crazy. She focused all of her power on Greg's body. He was too heavy to fully stop with her mind, but she managed to slow his fall just before she caught him. He slammed into her open arms, and they dropped down to absorb the weight. He narrowly missed hitting the concrete.

Everyone watching wouldn't have noticed it. She'd managed to slow his fall down enough to be able to handle his weight and catch him. She slowly lowered him to the ground. He lay there in shock, uninjured. Jessica was exhausted. Concentrating her powers on such a task and catching him was physically tough. The crowd of students started clapping.

"Did you see that? She caught him!" somebody shouted.

"That was amazing! He's so lucky," another added.

A few students were visibly shaken by what they'd witnessed. Jessica managed to slip away into the crowd. She moved through the sea of students and found a quiet area in the yard to sit. She needed to rest after the energy it took to slow Greg's fall and catch him.

That afternoon, as Jessica left through the front gate, Greg called to her, "Hey!"

She stopped walking, turned her head, and looked at him.

"Thanks," he said.

Jessica didn't say anything. She gave a slight nod. She started walking again.

That night, Jessica struggled to stay awake until the message that her driver was approaching came through. She was tired at training and just wanted to get home to sleep.

As Jessica was leaving training, Dalmar caught up with her in the carpark.

"You look tired," he said.

"I am. I just need to sleep."

Dalmar lowered his voice. "I need to talk to you. Can we meet tomorrow, out in front of your school? If you can hang around after school, I can get there twenty minutes after the bell?"

"Sure. See you then," Jessica said sleepily and walked off towards her driver's car. Zac saw her coming and started the engine.

Chapter 17: Dalmar's Trust

Jessica had been thinking all day at school about what Dalmar might want to discuss. *Did my way of stopping him reading my mind fail? Did he find out about Karim through my thoughts? Is Clint sending him to find out something?*

The end-of-day bell rang out across the school. Jessica walked to the front fence, near the main gate. She leaned against it and waited for Dalmar. She used her watch while she waited, memorising some new Japanese words. Over twenty minutes, lots of students headed home through the gate. Dalmar eventually showed up. His driver had brought him from Victor Bay to Lawson Primary. The car parked across from the school and down a little from the gate. Dalmar got out and crossed the street. As he walked towards Jessica, she left the school grounds to meet him.

"You're allowed to use the car for this kind of stuff? I thought it was just for going to the training centre?" Jessica asked.

"Yeah. Sometimes I'll send a request for a driver. You're allowed to do that. As long as you don't do it too much, they won't start asking questions."

"What did you want to talk about?"

Dalmar motioned for her to follow him across the road. They crossed to where Dalmar's driver was parked and then wandered a little farther up the road. Jessica assumed this was so the driver didn't overhear the conversation.

"Okay. Clint was showing a man and woman some of our team training. You were on the other side of the room, so you may not have noticed them. They were only there for a short time. He was talking quietly with them about how skilled we all are, and that we've done many missions similar to what they'd need us to do," Dalmar explained. He went on, "I was practicing on the rock-climbing wall at the time. I pretended not to notice them as I climbed. But I concentrated on their thoughts. From what I was able to find out, they thought our team would be perfect to steal secret documents from their competitor. They run a weapons business and want to steal from other weapons makers. Their goal's to be the first to make a powerful and highly-mobile particle accelerator gun. I tried to read Clint's thoughts but only caught him thinking about cows in a paddock."

"Cows in a paddock?" Jessica laughed. She was concerned with what Dalmar had said, but couldn't help laughing at Clint's thoughts.

"Yeah, some people who know there may be mind-readers around often use a blocking technique. They repeat a thought over and over again. Something like sheep jumping a fence, or counting bricks in a wall. It blocks people like me reading any useful thoughts. But most people can't concentrate on it strongly enough or for long enough. Their minds are too weak and they get distracted. They end up stopping or thinking other thoughts at the same time as the cows or sheep or whatever. But Clint's very disciplined, so I've noticed he's very good at doing that blocking technique when I'm around."

"How do you know the man and woman's mission was a bad one? It might have been to steal something back that was stolen from them?" Jessica suggested, trying to better understand what Dalmar may have uncovered.

"I tried to think the best of it too. But then I overheard Clint talking with Frank about communications needed for the potential mission, if it happens. Clint told him the mission was to help a government agency. To stop an evil weapons company making a new particle ray gun. I've had a feeling Clint was lying to us in the past about different missions. This time he was definitely lying to Frank."

Jessica had to decide how much she trusted Dalmar. Should she tell him about the research she did? What she'd found when searching galleries online? She decided to tell him.

"After our mission to get back the stolen ruby, I did some research. I found there were no galleries displaying or holding a double rose cut ruby in their collection. Seems Clint must have lied to us. But I've only been on the team for a short time. I've only been on one mission. I didn't know what to do about it," Jessica said. She stopped short of telling Dalmar about Karim and how she'd discussed the ruby mission with him.

"I've been in the team for a while, and there are a few things that just don't add up," Dalmar admitted. "Others may have noticed them too but just enjoy the money too much to question what we're really doing."

"What are you going to do now?" Jessica asked.

"I trust you, Jessica. I wanted to tell you about what happened last night. I wanted to tell you that I really don't trust Clint, and I don't want to be part of doing the wrong thing. I think that's what our team is probably doing ... on every mission."

"But even if we are, what can we do about it? It doesn't seem like we can leave the team. My dad had been struggling to find a job for ages. He needed to find something flexible enough to still look after my mum who's unwell. Just after I joined the team, he found the perfect job. Turns out, Clint's his boss," Jessica shared with Dalmar. Dalmar's eyes widened as Jessica continued, "The crazy thing is Dad's boss was dropping something over on the weekend and I opened the door.

There's Clint staring straight at me. He pretends he's only meeting me for the first time. And he calls himself Clive!"

"What? Clive?"

"Yeah. It's super weird. I just had to pretend he was Clive and go along with it. Last night at training he acted as if none of it happened. I think Clint set that job up for Dad somehow. I think it's to keep me locked into the team and stop me from leaving."

"Wow. It probably is. I think they've done similar things to others. Not exactly that, but other things that make it hard for people to leave, or even consider leaving."

"If we can't leave, what can we do?" Jessica wanted to see if Dalmar had thought through any options.

"Let's work out exactly what Clint's up to. Let's discover how these clients find out about Clint and our team. We can gather all the info and then work out what to do with it," Dalmar suggested.

"I may have somebody you'd be interested in meeting." Jessica figured she could trust Dalmar now. "He's part of that other team we came across when we were stealing the ruby."

"Oh? I'm so glad I trusted you, Jessica. I wasn't sure who I could trust, but I knew it'd take more than just me to work out what was going on. And you've already made some progress for us."

"I'm glad you talked to me about all of this. I'll organise something where we can chat with the guy from the other team," Jessica said.

"That'd be great. I'd better go … otherwise my driver may report this conversation. I've heard it's okay for them to drive us around occasionally, but who knows what they have to do? They always seem so cool and friendly, but perhaps they're just another way for Clint to keep track of us," Dalmar said.

"See you soon." Jessica turned to walk home.

Chapter 18: Now or Never

Jessica sat down. The first lesson of the day was starting shortly, and kids were filtering into the classroom. The space was loud with conversations and the sound of books and stationery being moved around. Jessica looked over at Tessa and smiled. Tessa seemed upset as she got up and approached Jessica.

"I saw you talking to that guy yesterday. When I left the stadium, after basketball training, I saw you. You were so into what he was saying, you didn't even notice me walking past," Tessa said.

"Oh, that was just Dalmar. You know. He was just saying hi," Jessica replied, trying to downplay the situation.

"What were you talking about?"

"He was just going on about his school. He has people giving him a hard time too. Like Greg and Chloe, but they sound worse," Jessica lied.

"Don't lie to me. I know when you're lying. Don't forget, I can read minds," Tessa warned.

Jessica froze for a moment. Her brain tried to process what she'd just heard. Then she remembered Tessa would sometimes say that if she thought somebody was lying to her. She couldn't really read minds. Up to this point, Jessica would have laughed at anyone who said they could. But after the last few weeks, with the people she'd met, she was less likely to take it as a joke.

"You're right," Jessica admitted. "I was actually talking to Dalmar about something really important. I want to tell you all about it. But I just can't, yet."

Tessa looked at Jessica like a child who'd just lost their favourite toy. She moved back to her seat and waited for class to start.

Students flooded the yard at the start of their lunch break. Greg took the opportunity to search out Jessica. He walked up to her.

"Hey," he started.

"What do you want?" Jessica replied.

"On Monday when I said thanks, you basically ignored me."

"Why should I be grateful that you said thanks after being mean for so long? All I had to do was save you from hitting hard concrete and you finally see me as a human being? How about you use whatever brain you have in that skull and have a long think about it?" Jessica unleashed. *Wow! I really stood up for myself!*

Greg was lost for words. Silently, he turned and walked away.

The end-of-day bell sounded. Jessica sighed with relief. It'd been a horrible day. Greg's attitude had upset her. Even worse, she was feeling terrible about lying to Tessa. *I need to avoid Tessa asking me about what's going on until I've met with Dalmar and Karim. Then I should be able to tell her everything. Or do I tell her now? What difference will it make? Nah, I should wait. Then I can explain what the three of us are going to do next.*

"There you are!" Tessa said, tapping Jessica on the shoulder as she walked.

"Hi, Tessa." Jessica stopped at the front fence beside the main gate. Students steadily streamed past the two girls.

"I need to know what's going on. I feel like you don't trust me. I feel excluded, and I don't deserve to be left out … because I always share everything with you," Tessa said, her emotion clearly building while she spoke.

"Tessa, I'll explain everything. I just need to talk to a couple of people first. But I promise I'll tell you everything," Jessica pleaded.

"Now or never."

"Please … just a couple of days. I need a couple of days," Jessica insisted.

Tessa's cheeks were red, her breathing was rapid, and her fists were clenched. She shrugged her right shoulder to reposition her schoolbag and walked through the school gate. Jessica followed, trying to calm her down.

"Please, Tessa. Stop," Jessica begged her friend. It only made things worse.

"Leave me alone!" Tessa shouted. She broke into a run and began to cross the road.

"Wait! Look out!" Jessica screamed.

Tessa swung her head around and saw a car. She froze like a deer caught in the headlights. Her eyes widened, and her mouth opened, but no sound came out.

The driver was distracted, looking down at his phone. He looked up in terror, seeing the young girl standing directly in front of his car. Precious time was lost as he moved his foot from the accelerator to the brake.

Jessica rushed forward. She was standing in the gutter, right at the edge of the road. Without thinking, she raised her hands towards the car. She quickly focused her mind on the car and summoned her power. She slammed her power towards the car like she was wrestling some imaginary beast.

The next few seconds felt like they were in slow motion. The sound of tyres screeching ripped through the air. The grinding and scraping of twisting metal pierced the ears of those now looking at the chilling scene play out. A few metres away, the crossing supervisor had dropped his sign and was running towards Tessa. Children were staring as the noise rang out. Some screams and squeals could be heard from those witnessing the nightmarish scene.

The car stopped a few centimetres from Tessa's shaking body. The back of the car left the ground and thumped back down a second later. There was a strong smell of rubber from the tyres. The driver was in shock.

Jessica collapsed on the sidewalk, exhausted from stopping such a fast, heavy object. She tried to lift her head but immediately felt dizzy and laid back down.

The driver rushed from his vehicle to check on Tessa. He got to her at the same time as the crossing supervisor.

"I didn't see her! She came out of nowhere," the driver exclaimed.

"Lucky you braked in time. You were so close to hitting her. It's amazing you didn't," the crossing supervisor replied.

"I don't even remember braking. I don't even remember it," he murmured, still clearly in shock.

They both knelt down next to Tessa, who had fallen to the ground.

"Are you okay?" the driver asked her. "Can you hear me?"

Tessa looked up at him, her eyes wide. She nodded slightly.

As students regained their senses, they started moving again. There was lots of noise. Some kids cried from what they'd just witnessed. Others were trying to make sense of it with their friends.

"Look, she's on the ground!" one girl called, staring at Jessica.

"Are you okay?" another asked as he tapped Jessica on the shoulder.

Jessica slowly lifted her head and sat up. She looked over to see Tessa getting to her feet. Jessica was overwhelmed with relief seeing that her best friend was safe. She shut her eyes and breathed deeply. She sucked in as much air as she could, and her body shook as she slowly exhaled.

Tessa's initial shock had worn off. She ran to Jessica and hugged her. Jessica wrapped her arms around Tessa.

"I'm so glad you're alright," Jessica said in a breathy whisper.

"Thanks to you."

Jessica removed her arms from around Tessa and straightened her back. "What?" she asked, almost instinctively.

"I saw something. I looked away from the car, and I saw you do something with your hands. Next thing, the car stopped and you collapsed. I don't know what happened, but you did something. That car was going way too fast to stop where it did."

"Are you okay? You're not injured?" Jessica asked. "If not, let's get you home, and I'll explain everything."

"Do we need to call an ambulance for either of them?" the driver asked another teacher, who was now on the scene. "That other one collapsed on the sidewalk."

"Ah, yes. They're friends. She was probably in shock seeing her friend almost get run over," the teacher reasoned. "They seem okay now. We can take it from here. But are you alright to drive?"

"Yeah. I'm okay now. Thank you," the driver replied.

Several other cars had pulled up behind the driver and were looking at the chaotic scene. The driver got back in his car and slowly drove away, the other cars following.

After convincing multiple teachers they were okay, Tessa and Jessica began to walk to Tessa's house.

The two girls didn't say much for most of the walk. They were still dealing with the shock of what had happened. There was a strange calm between them. There was an unspoken understanding that once they got to Tessa's house, Jessica would explain everything that had been going on.

The girls sat on Tessa's bed. Jessica looked over at Tessa's music player and nodded at it.

Tessa turned on some music.

Jessica leaned in and glanced over to Tessa's bedroom door. It was shut, but Jessica checked to see if anyone was standing on the other side. When she saw it was clear under the door, she began.

"Everything I'm about to tell you is the total truth," Jessica promised. "Some of it will be hard to believe, but I swear it's the truth."

As Jessica explained everything, starting with how she discovered her special powers, Tessa listened keenly. She didn't shake her head, laugh, or show any signs of doubting what her friend was telling her. She was totally supportive and gave Jessica the time to fully explain everything. Jessica explained how she met Dalmar and was recruited into Clint's team. She explained the mission to steal the ruby. She explained how Karim was also part of a team. She left no detail out. Jessica had not told Tessa the truth in the past. Now, she wanted to make sure Tessa knew everything. Deep down, she always knew Tessa would support her. At this point, it was safer for Tessa to know the truth about everything than not.

"Watch very carefully. See that book over there?" Jessica asked.

Tessa looked over at her study desk. There was a book sitting away from the rest of her papers and stationery. Jessica's face showed her concentration as she stared at the book. Nothing happened. Jessica raised her hands towards the book and narrowed her eyes. Still, nothing happened. The book didn't move a bit. Tessa looked at Jessica, confused.

"But I saw you stop that car. That's a lot harder than moving a little book," Tessa said.

Just then, the book lifted from the table and spun slowly in the air. Tessa looked on in amazement. She smiled, overcome with a sense of wonder. She was witnessing real magic in the middle of her bedroom. The book then returned to the desk, a lifeless object once again.

"I'm not sure what happened ... why that was so hard. I do still feel weak after stopping the car," Jessica explained.

"It's amazing!" Tessa exclaimed. "Absolutely amazing."

"I'd better get home. I'm meant to help with a few things before dinner. Just before I go … if Karim joins Dalmar and me to find out the truth behind everything—Clint, the teams, the clients—do you want to be part of it?"

"Totally," Tessa confirmed immediately. "And I have the perfect clubroom. Every team needs a clubroom. We have that under-house storage room with some junk in it. I can clean it up for us."

"That'd be awesome," Jessica said excitedly. "I'll see Dalmar at the training centre tomorrow night. I'll try to line up a group chat with him and Karim on Friday night. Are you doing anything Friday?"

"Nope. Not that I've heard."

"Okay. I'll see you tomorrow at school. I'll let you know about Friday night too, as soon as I know if the others can make it," Jessica said. Her mind was racing. *It'd be the ultimate to have the four of us become a team. Having a great clubroom to meet in would be such a bonus. Tessa's storage room's a good size and much better than meeting in a bedroom.*

Chapter 19: The Four

It was Friday. Jessica bounced out of bed. She was eager to get to school and share the good news with Tessa. Yesterday, she'd lined up Karim to meet tonight. She then saw Dalmar at their team's Thursday night session. She spent most of the night distracted, waiting for a short break to ask him if he'd meet her and the others. He was keen. Now it was Friday, and she wanted to update Tessa and line her up for the night too.

As soon as Tessa sat down at her desk, Jessica rushed over. "I've got Dalmar and Karim coming over to my place at seven tonight. I told my parents we'll be working on a school project. I don't think they'll know Dalmar's not from our school, so it should be okay. Can you make it to my place by then?"

"For sure. This is going to be so cool. I can't wait for them to read my mind and memories."

"Tessa, it's not as fun as it seems. It's a bit weird having people read *all* of your thoughts ... not just the ones you want or expect them to read."

"Oh. Yeah. I guess it could be a little weird. Anyway, I'm still excited."

Karim was first to arrive at Jessica's house. He lived a short walk away.

"Hey, Karim. Come in," Jessica welcomed him.

They walked to her room. Jessica had cleared a space in the corner and laid out four cushions for seats. As soon as they sat down, Tessa arrived.

Tim had sensed something exciting going on, so he'd been hanging around the living room and front door. He rushed to answer the knock.

"Oh, it's just you," he said as he saw Tessa standing there. "Come in. There's already some other dude in Jessica's room."

Tessa sat on a cushion in the corner with the others. They spent a few minutes chatting about school. Instinctively, they knew they had to chat about regular, boring things for a little while until Tim lost interest in why they were all meeting up. It didn't take long for another knock at the door. Jessica raced to answer it, but Tim was quicker.

"Hey, mate. I'm Dalmar," Dalmar introduced himself to Tim.

"Hi," Tim replied.

"Come to my room," Jessica interrupted, rushing to greet her guest.

The four of them sat quietly as Jessica shut her door. She carefully placed some folded clothes along the gap at the bottom of the door to stop anyone from overhearing their conversation.

"This is Dalmar," Jessica began. "Dalmar, this is Tessa and Karim. Let's start with why we're all here. Dalmar helped Clint recruit me into their secret team of kids with powers. On our recent mission, Karim and his team turned up. Karim and I both think our teams are dodgy and our coaches are lying to us. Dalmar thinks the same. We're all here to try and uncover the truth. Oh, and Tessa's been my best friend for years. I've told her everything, and she'd be an awesome part of the team. She's a tech wiz, which'll really help."

Dalmar straightened his back. "These teams recruit us. They use us to go on dangerous missions and make big money for themselves. They throw us a few crumbs. They muck with our lives … trying to control us. Well, they're messing with the wrong people. The reason they wanted us on their teams will be the same reason we become their worst nightmare. We're no ordinary kids …"

Jessica jumped back in, "Clint can't find out about the four of us working together. My dad can't afford to lose his job. It'll probably happen if Clint catches me doing anything he doesn't like. Clint has to think everything's just going along as normal."

"My team's coach, Oksana, can't find out about me either," Karim added. "She'd kill me … literally, I think."

"We might need to use code words and other ways to make sure nobody finds out?" Tessa suggested. "And we need somewhere we can meet and plan stuff."

"We can't wear our watches when we meet," warned Dalmar. "Clint and others could be using them to track us. They'll get suspicious if they see we're always hanging out together."

"Best to leave them at home," said Karim. "I'll leave the phone Oksana gave me at home too."

"Where are we going to meet?" Dalmar asked, bringing the conversation back to an earlier point.

"How about the storage room under my house?" Tessa suggested, looking at Jessica knowingly. "It's big, and I can shove Dad's junk somewhere else. Mum would be happy to throw most of it out. I can fix it up, and there's even an old couch in there we can use."

"Sounds amazing!" Karim said enthusiastically.

"Do you live far from here?" Dalmar asked. He was the only one who didn't live in Lawson and would have to travel the farthest.

"I'm pretty close to the shopping centre," Tessa replied.

"You know what … I'll get taxis if we're meeting at night. If it's in the day, I can jump on a bus,"

Dalmar said. "I'll definitely avoid using Clint's drivers. They'll report it if I keep getting driven to the same place. I've got enough money that taxis aren't a big deal."

"Awesome. Let's try and set up the clubroom as soon as we can," Jessica said.

Tessa gave her a smile. "Come around tomorrow. I'll start working on it in the morning. Then we can finish it when you get here."

"Perfect," Jessica replied.

"Actually, you guys can drop in too if you like," Tessa offered, looking at both Dalmar and Karim. "Maybe around four o'clock if you can? Everything should be finished by then. We can have our first team meeting."

"I'm in," Karim responded immediately.

"Me too," Dalmar added.

That night, Jessica felt a tingly happiness. She felt Christmas Eve and night-before-birthday feelings mixed into one. *The four of us make a great team. It*

feels good to be part of something important. I'm so
glad Tessa knows all about it now.

Chapter 20: The Clubroom

Tessa opened the door to Jessica. "Come in. I'll show you what I've done. I've been working on it all morning." Tessa took her through the house and into the backyard.

There was a door from the garden to access the under-house storage area. Tessa opened it and proudly showed Jessica her morning's efforts. It was impressive. All of her dad's junk had been cleared out. There were posters on the walls that flipped around to become writing surfaces. It was like having hidden whiteboards that could be used to plan missions and then be flipped back to hide them. A table tennis table took up a lot of space near the middle of the room. Tessa pointed out that under it, there were secret storage areas at each end. An old couch Tessa's family no longer used was at the far end of the room. Near it, were several other small stools and chairs. To one side of the couch and chairs was a cupboard and a set of drawers with a small music system sitting on top of it. Tessa had loaded the cupboard with snacks and the drawers with stationery. To the other side of the sitting area were a few crates. Tessa had filled them with equipment like torches, a first aid kit, as well as a bunch of random things like hooks, clips, small bags, and bottles.

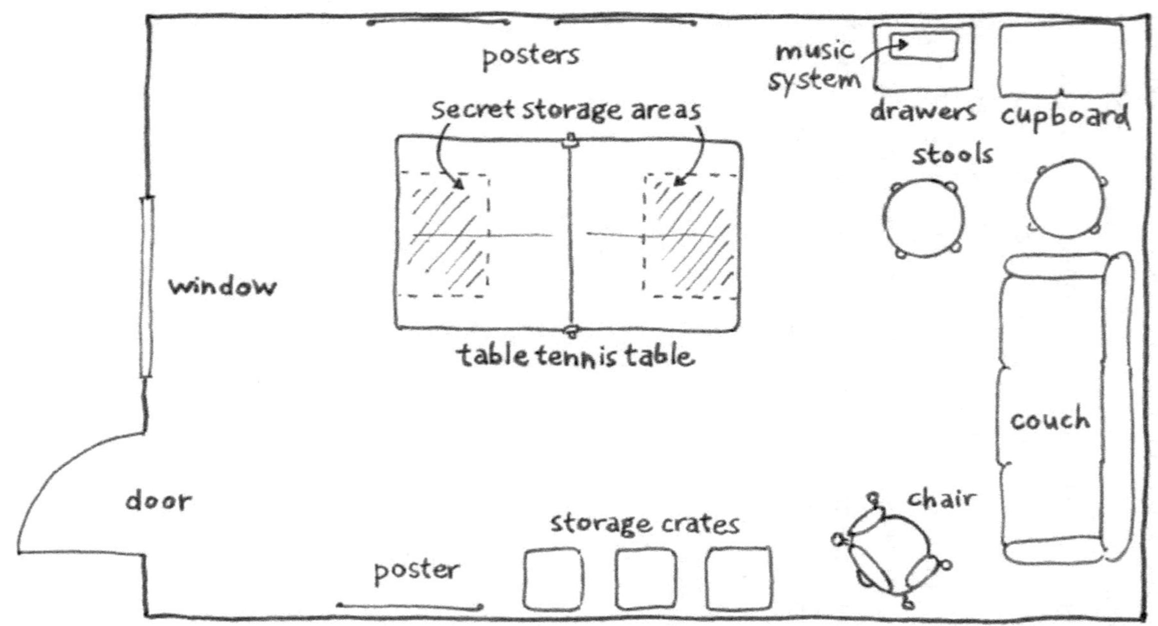

posters
music system
drawers
cupboard
Secret storage areas
stools
window
couch
table tennis table
door
chair
storage crates
poster

"This is super impressive," Jessica complimented Tessa.

"I think I basically finished it all this morning. There really isn't much left to do. We can relax and wait for the guys."

"Tessa, your friend's here!" her mum called, poking her head out the back door.

"Okay!" Tessa left Jessica relaxing on the couch and went inside the house.

Tessa opened the door to see Karim beaming at her.

"Hi, Tessa."

"Hey, Karim. We might as well wait here for Dalmar to show up before we head out back."

It was only a few minutes before Dalmar came walking up to the others.

"Hi, you two," Dalmar said cheerily.

Tessa took them through the house, out the back door, and around to the clubroom.

"Hey, how's it going Jessica?" Dalmar began. "Wow! Tessa, this place is amazing!"

"Yeah, this is unbelievable," Karim agreed, looking around the room.

The boys explored the details of the space, finding the snacks and stationery straight away. Tessa showed them the secret storage areas and the hidden writing surfaces behind the posters.

Karim took his backpack from his shoulder and unzipped it. He handed Tessa three packs of biscuits and a box of candies.

"This should help stock up that snacks cupboard a bit," he said.

"Thanks, Karim." Tessa placed them into the cupboard.

Jessica and Dalmar sat on the couch. Karim wheeled over a chair, and Tessa dragged a stool in close. The four spent some time dreaming up extra things to fill the clubroom with. They talked about who'd probably be the best table tennis player. They briefly talked about designing team uniforms, before dismissing the idea. Then they sat quietly, enjoying a moment together as a new team, in their new clubroom.

Jessica let her mind wander. *What a crazy couple of months. I had a power I couldn't really use for much. My family was struggling. I was getting bullied most days. Then I joined a top-secret group of kids like me. Now I make more money than I could have dreamed of making. I've learnt new skills … I can fight with sai, hit targets with throwing stars, pick locks, and I'm even starting to speak Japanese! I've found out the team I'm in is probably dodgy. I've saved lives. Now I'm in a new team of awesome friends, searching for the truth about these dodgy, top-secret groups. I'm not afraid of anything anymore. I'm stronger now than I ever imagined I could be.*

Jessica smiled slightly as she looked around at the others. She broke the silence …

"Hey, team … time for the biggest adventure of our lives!"

To be continued …

About the Author

Andrew Hobday (BA, MIntl&CommunityDev, MCommLaw) was born and raised in Melbourne, Australia.

He has a passion for storytelling. In his corporate career he uses business storytelling to engage and educate everyone from executives and colleagues to conference attendees and other external audiences.

He writes and speaks on the topic of *business agility* and is currently working on a book exploring the psychology of *business agility*.

Known for his creative stories, metaphors and analogies, he's carried these through into the realm of fiction for younger readers. He enjoys stepping away from business topics, to create contemporary children's and upper middle-grade books.

Website: www.businessagilitycentral.com

www.ingramcontent.com/pod-product-compliance
Lightning Source LLC
Chambersburg PA
CBHW061253120726
48001CB00001B/291